LUCKY CHARM IN LAS VEGAS

A.R. WINTERS

Do you believe in luck?

Uptight accountant Andrew Coombs has no time for superstitions – until he meets his own personal Lady Luck, Charlene Nelson, the lovely casino waitress who helps him win big at the slots. But when Charlene stands him up on a date night, Lady Luck is no longer on his side – or in the land of the living.

Who would kill the cocktail waitress? Who was Charlene Nelson when she wasn't slinging drinks? Out-of-towner Andrew doesn't have a clue where to start looking for answers…

As luck would have it, Ian and Tiffany are on the scene – though this time, their murder investigation plays second fiddle to an even bigger and incredibly dangerous operation.

Tiffany's friend Stone is out to clear his

name and prove his innocence. When war refugee Tariq Zubair knocks on Tiffany's door, the final puzzle piece is nearly in place.

But dark forces lurk in the background and want the truth to stay buried at all costs, even if that means burying Tiffany and Ian along with it! Can the sleuths solve the mystery without becoming a statistic them-selves? And can Stone finally come back into Tiffany's life for good?

PROLOGUE

*A*ndrew Coombs walked into the pit of the Treasury casino.

It was an exciting place, with bright lights, gaudy carpets, and a flamboyant, happy vibe. People of all ages, shapes and ethnicities milled about the floor—most of them were dressed in vacation clothes, but a few were dressed up, as if they were going out to a fancy dinner. Come to think of it, maybe some of them were going to dinner right after this, or maybe they'd hit up a show.

Andrew took it all in and smiled bravely. The pit was loud, almost over-whelmingly so, but he wouldn't let that deter him. He took a deep breath, and inched his way forward.

This was his first time in Vegas.

Andrew had checked in at the casino a little while back. He'd booked into one of the cheapest rooms he could find, but he hadn't been disappointed—the room was a decent size, and had a sparkling clean feeling. His window overlooked the windows of another building across the street, but he didn't mind; he'd hardly be in his room, he told himself.

Andrew was twenty-nine years old, and for the first time in his life, he was going to have fun.

He made his way over to the circular bar in the middle of the pit. Before he could stop himself, he ordered a soda with lime, and then realized his mistake. The bartender, a pretty young woman with long, straight black hair had gone off to mix his drink, so it was too late to change his order.

No more soda-limes in Vegas, he told himself. He was here to have fun—and didn't people order lots of alcohol when they wanted to have fun?

"First time in Vegas?" asked a woman who'd sidled onto a seat next to him.

Andrew looked at her and nodded. "Just landed."

The woman seemed to be in her early forties. She was plump, with puffy cheeks reddened by make-up. Her blond hair seemed artificially fluffed out, and her lips were glittering red. Something about the woman made Andrew shrink back, but she didn't seem to notice.

"My name's Myra," she said. "I come here all the time."

Andrew didn't quite know what to say. He'd never been much of a talker, and when his drink arrived, he sipped it and pulled out his cell phone. He didn't feel like talking to Myra, and he checked his email. There were a few from the office, and Andrew decided he might as well reply to them.

"I can't believe you're working on vacation," Myra said from beside him. Her drink, something red and sparkly in a tall

A.R. WINTERS

glass, arrived. "Aren't you here to have some fun?"

Andrew turned and looked at her. "I am. Just as soon as I finish up my work."

Myra rolled her eyes. "I know guys like you. Your work never stops."

Myra seemed to notice someone, and waved in their direction, before grabbing her glass and sliding off.

Andrew followed her with his eyes—she was heading over to meet a group of three other women who looked eerily similar to her—puffed out faces, bright make-up, and fake-looking hair.

With a sinking heart, Andrew noticed that almost everyone in the casino was here with someone else. There were couples, and large groups of friends. The few single people seemed to quickly meet up with others, and they all laughed and chatted and relaxed into their surroundings.

Andrew, on the other hand, felt stiff and uneasy. It was probably time to start hitting the alcohol.

Just when Andrew was about to place an order for some kind of stiff drink—some

4

cocktail, he decided, because wasn't that what people ordered on vacation?—a young man plopped down onto the seat Myra had vacated.

The man turned and grinned at Andrew. He had a large shock of curly red hair, freckled skin, and dancing green eyes.

"I hope this seat isn't taken," the young man said.

Andrew shook his head. Something about the man made him feel at ease, like he wasn't an intruder in this happy space. "No, I'm just here by myself."

The bartender came over, and the man next to Andrew ordered a beer. "I'm here by myself too," he said, when the bartender left to get his beer. "I'm supposed to meet a friend of mine, who works here as a dealer. Her shift ends in a bit. My name's Ian."

"Andrew."

The two shook hands, and then Ian said, "How come you're here by yourself? Most of the tourists come in packs. Like wolves."

Ian grinned and laughed at his own joke, and Andrew found himself joining in with the laughter. The joke wasn't funny, but Ian's laugh was infectious.

"I was supposed to come with a bunch of friends," Andrew said. "It was Tony's bachelor party. But then the wedding got called off, so the bachelor party got canceled. I decided to come by myself anyway."

Ian tapped his forehead with one finger. "Smart thinking. Never miss a trip to Vegas."

"It's my first time, actually." When the bartender came with Ian's beer, Andrew took the plunge and ordered himself a martini. Wasn't that what James Bond drank? "I never really managed to take a proper vacation before this."

Ian turned and looked at him with interest. "Too busy working?"

Andrew nodded. Ian was easy to talk to, and his green eyes were sympathetic. The story of Andrew's life came flooding out. "I was the first in my family to go to college— I got a scholarship, but it only covered tuition. So I had to work nights at a restaurant to cover my dorm fees. When all the college kids were out having fun, I was either studying so that my scholarship didn't get canceled, or working nights at the restaurant."

"And then you got a job," Ian supplied.

"Yeah. And then my parents died. I didn't know what else to do, so I kept working hard. I saved up some money, and I invested a bit, and I got promoted. And then somehow, I became the guy with no life. Everyone kept sending their work my way—not that I'm complaining. I did okay. I got a promotion or two, and now I make decent money."

Ian grinned. "And now it's time to have some fun."

Andrew's martini arrived, and he took a sip. At client functions, he made sure to only drink red wine. Now, Andrew wasn't sure if he actually liked the martini or not. "For a few days," Andrew said. "After that, it's back to work."

"What do you usually do on vacations?"

"I've been buying some rundown properties to invest in. If I ever take time off work, I oversee those, and manage the tenants."

Ian looked at Andrew appraisingly. "All work and no play…"

Andrew smiled. "Well I'm here now. I might take a few days off work every year from now on. If this vacation goes well, that is."

Ian nodded. "What's your work?"

Andrew took a big gulp of his martini. "I'm an accountant," he said sheepishly. For some reason, admitting to being a boring person who crunched numbers all day seemed embarrassing in this fun-filled place. "I know it sounds boring, but I guess it suits me."

Ian smiled and nodded. His tone was friendly as he said, "It's a job, not a life. Not everyone wants to be a daredevil when they grow up."

Andrew smiled with relief. "Exactly." This young man seemed to understand him.

Despite being embarrassed about it, Andrew fit the stereotype of an accountant —he believed in numbers, he believed in logic, and he believed in hard work. Hard work seemed like a taboo concept these days, but Andrew still believed in it. A lot of his college classmates had wanted success to just drop into their laps, and had laughed at Andrew's lack of an exciting life.

Ian looked off to his right, and something caught his eye. He took a large swig of his beer, and said, "I can see my friend now—her shift must be over. I'll see you around."

"Hopefully," Andrew said. "I think I like this bar. You can see almost all of the casino pit from here."

The two men said goodbye, and then Ian jumped off his seat, and rushed toward a young woman wearing jeans and a T-shirt.

Andrew shrugged his shoulders. He'd probably never see Ian again, but at least the man had made him feel as though coming to Vegas by himself hadn't been a big mistake.

The night still had promise, and Andrew was determined to have a good time. Just because he was a boring accountant at home didn't mean he would be boring in Vegas.

It was time to shed his skin, and try something different.

❧

Once Ian left, Andrew turned up and emptied his drink, and headed toward the Craps table.

That seemed to be the center of the action—a throng of people gathered around, cheering and whooping each time the dice were rolled. But big crowds, especially loud ones, made Andrew nervous. After two steps in that direction, he hesitated and watched the table. A few seconds later, the whoops stopped, and people slowly started leaving the table. The throws of the dice seemed to have become unfavorable.

Andrew decided to take that as a sign. He didn't believe in signs—he believed in logic and math. But since the casino didn't seem like a place that embraced math and logic, he half-heartedly decided to take a stab at believing in luck.

But not too big a stab, just a little nick. Andrew decided that a slot machine, where he could spend a dollar or two trying to make back a few more dollars, was just what he needed to ease into gambling.

He headed toward a section of the floor that seemed dedicated to slot machines, and glanced around timidly. The young people, the crowd who seemed far too cool for folks like him, were nowhere to be seen in this part of the casino. Instead, a middle-aged couple chatted and laughed, and a kindly-looking woman with curly white hair smiled at him.

Andrew picked his slot machine, and stared at it nervously. It was no big deal. He just needed to spend a dollar, and even if he lost, it wouldn't be a big deal.

Before he inserted his token, a pretty girl in a cocktail waitress uniform appeared by side. "Would you like a drink?" she said.

Andrew was going to say no—he wasn't a big drinker, and he'd already had one martini tonight. But the girl's voice was sweet and lilting, and he turned to look at her.

She was a petite, skinny young thing, wearing high heels and lots of make-up. Her blond hair was pulled back, and Andrew could see the dark roots showing through. There seemed to be something naïve and innocent about her, and Andrew smiled.

"I would like a drink," he said. "I'm a bit nervous about my luck."

"What would you like?"

"A martini," Andrew said, deciding to stick with the same drink for tonight.

"Coming up, James Bond," the girl said with a smile. She fluttered her eyelids at him, and disappeared.

When the girl reappeared and started walking toward him with his drink, Andrew finally inserted the token. To his surprise, a trio of cherries lined up on the screen, and a celebratory tune rang out.

Andrew turned to the girl in surprise and took the proffered drink. "I can't believe it! I've never been lucky in my entire life."

The girl's eyes twinkled. Her nametag said Charlene, and she glanced at the screen.

"You won ten dollars," she said, smiling at Andrew politely. "Maybe your luck will continue tonight."

Andrew took a large swig of his drink. "I think you're my lucky charm. I've never been lucky, but now that you've appeared, things seem to have changed."

Charlene shrugged modestly. "Are you sure I'm your lucky charm? It's only ten dollars. If you really feel lucky, you should try the big shooter slot machine up in front. The main prize is five hundred thousand dollars."

Andrew raised one eyebrow. That was a few times his annual salary—what would he do if he won that money?

The logical Andrew would buy a few more investment properties; perhaps the lucky Andrew would quit his job, move to Vegas, and become a professional gambler. He grinned to himself. What an appealing dream.

"If you really are my lucky charm,"

Andrew said, "I can't just let you get away, or all my luck will be gone."

"But maybe I'm not your lucky charm."

"Why don't I try the slot machine," Andrew said, "and if I win the five hundred thousand dollars, we can go out for a drink after your shift ends. What do you say?"

Charlene giggled. "Sure, if you win the five hundred thousand."

Andrew downed his martini quickly, and rushed over to the slot machine Charlene had pointed out. He took a deep breath —he'd never believed in luck before. But tonight—ever since he'd met Charlene— there seemed to be something in the air. He hadn't had time to date in college, and since getting a job, he'd never been in a serious relationship. Perhaps now that he'd met Charlene, that would change.

Andrew inserted his token in the slot machine, and held his breath as the images spun before him.

Slowly, they stopped moving. As if in a dream, Andrew saw the three cherries line up in one straight row.

A jingle began to play. It sounded like

falling coins, interspersed with whoops and cheers. A crowd began to gather around Andrew, and he turned around, scanning the distance for Charlene. Their eyes met, and Andrew grinned happily.

A date with Charlene would be worth far more than the prize money he'd just won.

CHAPTER 1

*M*y shift had been uneventful—well, at least uneventful compared to my last few shifts when fistfights had broken out, two drunk men had vomited all over the casino rug, and a woman had walked up to her husband, thrown a Cosmopolitan in his face, and accused him of having an affair with the svelte brunette on his arm.

I made a quick pit-stop at the employee locker room, where I changed out of my red and black dealer's uniform and into a tunic top and leggings. I grabbed my large tote bag, and headed out of the employees' room and over to the lobby of the Treasury Casino. I was a few paces away from the main entrance when I spotted my friend Ian lounging in one of the oversized leather armchairs.

He was sunk back in the chair, looking half-asleep as his eyes drifting lazily across the sea of people.

I hadn't been expecting to see him tonight, and for a split second, I narrowed my eyes. Why was Ian here? Was something wrong? But Ian looked far too relaxed for anything to be wrong. Maybe he'd come to hang out at the casino like he sometimes does.

Ian is my neighbor and lives down the hall. We met a while back when I was on the run from a homicidal maniac, and since then, I haven't been able to shake him off.

At first, I'd found his perpetual enthusiasm and over-the-top excitement about life kind of irritating. Even more annoying was the fact that he insisted he wanted to be a private investigator, just like me, and he kept trying to tag along on cases.

But after we worked together on a few cases, I found myself getting used to his presence, and actually feeling grateful for his attempts at being a detective. Gradually, I started to think of Ian less as the annoying person I couldn't shake off, and more as the slightly immature younger brother I'd never really had.

My name is Tiffany Black, and I work as a private investigator. That is, when I'm not working as a dealer for the Treasury Casino.

Ian noticed me standing there, and bounded to his feet. His face split in a wide grin, and he strode over to me.

"Tiffany! I'm glad I ran into you."

"Not too hard to do," I said, "given how you knew that my shift was ending around this time."

As Ian and I headed out of the casino, I noticed a tall, slim blonde watching us. She would've blended into the mass of people who were in the casino, but she caught my eye because of her unusual outfit of sparkly purple leggings, purple tank top and long blond hair dyed with dark purple streaks. Our eyes met, and then she walked away toward the casino pit, merging back into the sea of people.

Ian glanced around. "The Treasury seems super busy for three AM on a Tuesday night."

"It is," I said, and for a few minutes, as we walked home, we chatted about the casino, and one of the previous cases we'd worked on.

I live a twenty-minute walk away from the Strip, and I almost always walk to and from work, given how traffic tends to grind to a halt at busy times.

As we headed back toward our apartment complex, Ian said, "Actually, part of the reason I wanted to meet up after your shift is because someone wants to hire us."

"You didn't have to come out to the casino to tell me that—you could've just told me tomorrow," I said. "What is it, another surveillance case?"

"No, it's another murder."

I groaned. "I've had enough of those cases. Especially that last one—I didn't like having to work on the same thing as my boyfriend."

My boyfriend, Ryan Dmitriou, was a detective with the LVMPD. That had been the first time we'd worked together on the same case, and while it had ended up being all right, I'd been worried there for a bit.

"I feel really bad for the man who wants to hire us," Ian said quickly. "I met him a few days back at the bar in the Treasury, and he seems like a super nice dude. He thought he'd have a fun time in Vegas, but instead, he fell in love with someone who got herself killed."

I raised one eyebrow cynically. "He fell in *love* with someone he met in Vegas?"

"A cocktail waitress at the Treasury."

I pressed my lips together. I'm not a believer in love at first sight—that kind of thing has never worked for me. And I'm even less of a believer when it comes to people who meet each other in Vegas. Most of the newly acquainted couples in this town seemed to believe in the old adage, "What happens in Vegas, stays in Vegas."

Stories of finding true love in this city are rare; here, it's more common to hear stories of getting hurt, getting a disease, or getting swindled.

"I tried to discourage him," Ian said,

looking serious. "But you know how it is when you suddenly fall madly in love."

Unlike me, Ian is a true romantic. He believes in falling in love quickly—and has the scars on his heart to prove it.

Ian's romantic issues are made worse by the fact that he's got a bit of money. When he was in college, Ian invested in a start-up that went on to do very well: Ian divested of his shares at just the right time and dropped out of college. His millions are held safely in a trust fund managed by his strict parents and a lawyer, which in my opinion is a good thing and has prevented Ian from blowing through all his money at once. Left to his own devices, Ian could burn through a couple million dollars in a month—not on himself, but on the kind of people who make a living by swindling others out of their hard-earned money.

Every time Ian meets a girl in Vegas, she quickly finds out about his money, and tries to get her hands on it. When she learns how strict Ian's parents are with the conditions of his trust fund and access to it, the girl quickly flees and finds a better target.

"Let me get this clear," I said. "You met a guy a few days ago at a bar. This guy met a cocktail waitress, and thinks he fell in love with her. The cocktail waitress then got killed. Am I getting the story straight so far?"

"Sort of."

I was about to ask Ian to tell me more, when I froze.

We were in a well-lit side street, almost halfway home. But I thought I'd heard something unusual for this time of night. My heart thudded loudly, and my senses sharpened.

"Do you hear footsteps?" I said under my breath.

Beside me, Ian stood very still. We looked around ourselves warily, but I couldn't see anyone.

"I wasn't paying attention," Ian said sheepishly. "Are you sure you heard something?"

I shook my head. "It might've just been

nerves. Ever since Stone told me that Tariq's about to show up..."

I let the words trail off. I didn't feel comfortable talking about Stone, Tariq and Eli in public, especially when I was worried that one of Eli's men might be nearby.

"I'm sure it's nothing," Ian said. "Have you seen anyone following you around?"

I started walking again, trying to calm my nerves, and shook my head. "No, but Stone told me to be careful. He thinks we're being watched—and I just can't shake the feeling there might be someone out there, lurking behind one of these parked cars."

I thought back briefly to my clandestine chat with Stone, just a few days ago when he'd warned me to be careful.

Stone and I had first met when we worked together on a case. He'd helped me learn a few tricks of the trade, and afterward, we'd stayed in touch and worked together a few more times. We'd been good friends until one night when we shared a passionate kiss.

That kiss had made me think things had changed between us—that perhaps our relationship would grow to be something serious.

But before I could act on my emotions, two dark-suited men from the CIA showed up at my front door, demanding to talk to him.

They claimed that Stone had betrayed his team while working in the CIA, and that they were there to track him down.

The CIA operatives' presence meant Stone went underground for a long time. I never once believed that Stone had betrayed his team, and I never stopped searching for answers—answers that I finally got from a man who called himself Johnson, who had been Stone's handler in the CIA.

Johnson told me that while Stone had been working undercover in Afghanistan, someone in his team had betrayed him— that man turned out to be Eli Cohen, a CIA operative who retired soon after the war in Afghanistan broke out, but still had powerful contacts within the agency.

Johnson and I spent a long time surveilling Eli and his men, and just when we'd been about to give up, we discovered that the third member of Stone's team in Afghanistan, an Afghan man named Tariq, was still alive and had escaped to a small village during the war. In fact, Tariq had recently made his way to the US.

After a while, we managed to get a message through to Tariq, letting him know that Stone needed his help—and now, Tariq was due to arrive in Vegas any day.

Stone had given Tariq my address, and told him that he'd be safe staying with either Ian or me. Unfortunately, my closeness with Stone had brought me onto Eli's radar—Stone had warned me that Eli and his men might be watching me.

Now, standing in the well-lit side street just after three in the morning, I worried that the footsteps I thought I heard were real—and that they belonged to Eli or someone working for him.

"I'm sure everything's fine," Ian said, trying to reassure me. But his voice sounded shakier than usual, and I knew he was nervous about a possible future run-in with Eli. "Eli or his men wouldn't come after you. They wouldn't want to draw attention to themselves that way."

"But it might not be drawing attention to themselves," I said reluctantly. "The police know I've received death threats from suspects I've investigated in the past. If anything happens to me they might think it's just someone from a case."

"Nothing's going to happen to you," Ian said stoutly. "I'll meet you at the casino every night from now on. If the two of us are together, no one'll attack us. Strength in numbers, right?"

I shook my head, not wanting to be a burden. "You don't have to do that."

"It's nothing. Besides, I get bored staying at home by myself watching Star Trek reruns. I need to get out sometimes, and if I'm alone, Eli and his men might attack me. I'd feel better if I was hanging out with you."

I glanced at Ian, wondering if he'd just come up with a clever excuse to be my bodyguard. But Ian didn't possess that level of cunning—with him, what you saw was what you got. And of course, I didn't want anything to happen to Ian.

"Maybe you're right," I admitted reluctantly. "There is strength in numbers. I guess we should stick together from now on."

A few minutes later, we were inside our apartment complex, and said goodbye to each other in the hallway.

I entered my small one-bedroom apartment, and locked the front door safely behind me. I checked through my apartment for intruders, the way Stone had shown me to do. When I was sure there was no one in there but me, I let out a large sigh of relief.

I didn't like stressing about Eli and his men all the time, but hopefully it would be worth it. Once Stone's issues with the CIA were sorted out, perhaps life would get back to normal.

CHAPTER 2

The next morning, I woke up around eleven, had a long, leisurely shower, and then texted Ian to see if he wanted to come over for a late brunch.

Ian showed up a few minutes later, carrying his kitten, Snowflake, with him.

Snowflake was a little bundle of white fur with bright blue eyes—Ian had rescued her when she was a tiny kitten, only slightly bigger than my hand. She's grown a little bit bigger now, but she's still adorable and heart-melting, and I'm always so glad to see her.

Ian and I played with Snowflake for a few minutes, and then I made us each a mug of steaming hot coffee. There was a rare carton of eggs in my fridge, along with some shredded cheese and sliced mush-rooms. I made Ian and myself each a massive omelet, and then we carried our food and coffees over to the sofa. We were just about to bite into our food when there was a loud knock on my door.

Ian turned to me and raised one eyebrow. "Were you expecting someone?"

"No, not at this hour."

"Maybe it's Ryan, here to surprise you with a sudden lunch date."

I glanced at the omelets. If that was the case, Ian could have my food too.

I opened the door and stared out in surprise. I think my jaw may have dropped slightly, and my eyes definitely grew wider.

I'd never seen the man before in my life, but I instantly knew who it was.

Tariq was tall, at least six feet two, with broad shoulders and olive skin. His hair and eyes were jet black, and his face was clean-shaven and square-jawed. He looked handsome and stylish in his chinos and checkered shirt; any red-blooded woman would have to be blind not to acknowledge that the man standing in front of me was gorgeous.

Why had I been expecting a man reminiscent of the Taliban, wearing some kind of white linen garb with a waist-length beard?

"You must be Tiffany Black," the man standing in my doorway said. He spoke with a slightly foreign accent, and I nodded silently.

I wasn't sure I could speak without stuttering, so I just stared silently, bug-eyed.

Tariq probably hadn't expected me to look so... downright tongue-tied. Hesitation flickered in his eyes. "My friend—he said you would be expecting me?"

I nodded rapidly, and glanced down the hall. There was nobody there.

"Come in," I said quickly.

When Tariq stepped inside, I made sure to lock the door behind us.

"This is my friend Ian," I said, "And that's Snowflake on top of the fridge."

Tariq sat down on a chair opposite us, and from her perch on top of the fridge, Snowflake opened one lazy eye. She glanced at the man, decided that her nap was over, and jumped off the fridge to head over to Tariq.

He made clucking sounds at the little kitten. "I love kittens! It is so nice to meet you, Snowflake."

Snowflake rubbed against Tariq's ankles, and he lifted her onto his lap. He stroked her fur gently and said, "Every cat has a unique personality. You never know what to expect. Almost like humans."

"But nicer than humans," Ian said.

Tariq smiled at him. "She is your cat?"

Ian looked surprised. "How did you know?"

Tariq gazed at Snowflake and scratched behind her ears. "When you have a pet, your heart opens up. You act differently—I can tell when someone has an animal they care for, and when someone does not."

I wondered if I should be offended. But then I figured he was right—I wasn't responsible for Snowflake, no matter how much I loved her. "Did you have a cat back in Afghanistan?"

"Yes, I had a lovely black cat with green

eyes. She was very independent." Tariq smiled at the memories.

"Did she… did you leave her behind?"

Tariq's expression grew serious again. "No, she passed away a year before I left the country. I still miss her. Losing a pet is losing a member of your family."

"I'm sorry," Ian said. "She must've been a good cat."

Tariq nodded. "Yes. And I like to think that she had a happy life."

I said, "I'm glad you made it in one piece."

Tariq smiled wryly. "I almost did not."

I nodded, wondering what to say to that. How do you respond to someone who's escaped a war-torn country?

Ian had no such tact. He said, "It must've been terrible in Kabul, with all that bombing and fighting going on."

Tariq nodded grimly. "It was horrible. Before the war, Stone, Eli and I all had covers as university professors, but when the Taliban took over, they shut down the university. Stone disappeared before the Taliban took over, and Eli told me that

Stone had betrayed us. I went underground, and Eli disappeared.

"I managed to stay hidden in my uncle's village while the war went on. Afterward when the American troops took over, I headed back to Kabul. I met a man who understood that I helped out before the war and the US Army brought me on as an interpreter. A few months ago, my application for an American green card was approved, and I came over to California."

"I'm surprised Eli hasn't found you before this," I said.

Tariq shook his head. "I have learned that sadly you can never be too careful. The American consulate advised me to come to the USA under an assumed name. So when I entered the country, I was Riyaz Husnei Ibrahim, not Tariq Zubair."

"So that's why Eli didn't know you were in the country for a long time."

Tariq nodded. "But then I met an American who had been in Kabul during the war and I admitted I had actually worked with the US government myself. That was a mistake—or maybe not. That conversation is how Eli found out I was in the country. But if I had not talked to that man, then you would not have found me either."

I nodded. "What tipped you off that Eli had been the one to betray you?"

Tariq smiled thinly. "After Stone disappeared, I knew that something was not right. I had never trusted Eli—something about him had always seemed... how do you say it? 'Off.' So one night, I went into his office room, and placed a key logger on his computer. Eli may be a clever man, but he never realized that his computer had been hacked. After that, I was able to see everything he did—I could see all his emails, all his correspondence with the Russian arms dealers. I am not so sure how he got away with it for such a long time, but I have made copies of all his documents. I have those copies with me now, on a flash drive."

I shivered involuntarily and slid my eyes toward the door. I couldn't hear any footsteps, so I looked at Tariq again.

I tried to ignore the sound of blood pounding in my ears, and took a deep breath. "So what you're saying is that you've got proof on you that Stone is completely innocent?"

"And that Eli was the one who betrayed us all along."

"Are you sure—"

Words failed me. I gawked at Tariq in silence.

"You need to be safe," Ian said, echoing my thoughts.

Tariq shrugged. "I do what I can."

I glanced at him sharply. If anyone else had said that, I would have thought they weren't taking the matter seriously enough. But this was a man who'd clearly survived multiple attempts on his life and who Stone trusted with his own life. I figured I should relax, and let Tariq take care of his own safety.

Stone... That reminded me. "You and Stone worked together for a while."

Tariq smiled and his face lit up. If he had looked handsome when he was being serious, he looked downright heart-stopping when he smiled.

"Stone and I have always been friends,"

he said. "I have learned to trust my instincts when it comes to people—it is what saved my life multiple times. Stone has something about him—something you can trust."

I nodded. I knew what he meant. "What was Stone like when you were working together?"

"I have not seen Stone since he disappeared. But he was younger than me. And he had not been to Afghanistan before. He wanted to help people, he wanted to make things right.

"I was old enough to know how the world worked. Politics is a dirty game, and when you have the opportunity to make lots of money, like Eli did, you do not care if other people get hurt. Even if those people getting hurt are those who live right next to you—even if your deals with an arms trader means that entire cities, young children and women and families get wiped out or hurt or tortured. Some people do not care. Some people do. Eli did not care at all about other people. All Stone cared about was other people, the people he could save."

The three of us sat silently for a few minutes, thinking about what Tariq must've been through. And Stone, too.

Johnson had told me that Stone had gotten into trouble by trying to save a young Afghan girl and her mother—I couldn't help but wonder who else Stone had managed to save without being detected.

"Anyway," Tariq said, smiling at Ian and me. "I am here now. If your friend Stone is in trouble, I am going to try to help him."

I could see why Stone trusted Tariq with his life. The man was a fan of under-statements, and just like Stone, there was something solid and dependable about him.

"You can stay in my apartment," Ian said quickly. "Eli will never think that you're staying with me—he didn't even know that Stone and I were friends."

Tariq said, "Will you be sending a message to Stone?"

Ian and I exchanged a glance.

"I have a way to get in touch with him," I said slowly. "I'll do that."

Tariq nodded seriously. He could see I

didn't want to admit all the details to him, not just yet. Nanna had once told me that walls have ears, and I believed in that adage now. After Stone had gone underground, I'd become extra cautious.

"You can head over to my apartment now," Ian said. "Unless you'd like to join us for brunch?"

Tariq shook his head no. "I ate on the drive over here. My car is parked downstairs. I only have a small duffel bag. I will get it now, and head over to your place. I assume it is better for me to stay indoors."

"I think so," I said slowly. "We need to make sure that Eli and his men don't find out that you're in Vegas—let alone that you're staying here with us."

CHAPTER 3

*A*fter Ian handed Tariq the key to his apartment, Tariq disappeared to get his bag and settle in at Ian's place, and I sent Stone a text to let him know the news.

I found a box of chocolate chip cookies in one of my kitchen cabinets; packet cookies tasted nothing like a good home-made cookie, but they would have to do in a pinch. They were thinner than home-made cookies, but they had a lovely crunch and just the right amount of dark chocolate chips. Ian and I chewed on them nervously.

"He's different from what I expected," Ian said. "He doesn't seem like a spy, or an Afghan."

I shrugged. "That's exactly what I thought. But I hope…" I took a deep breath, and forced myself to finish the sentence. "I hope everything works out. I hope Eli never finds out that Tariq is already here, and I hope Stone and he manage to get their work done."

Ian nodded and agreed, but as I thought about Eli and his men, my heart had started thudding loudly, and it still rang in my ears. We chewed our cookies anxiously, and then there was a knock on my door.

Ian turned to me. "That must be Andrew. I told him to come by around this time today to have a chat."

"I don't really feel like taking on a case now. I'm too nervous about this whole Tariq situation."

"It will be good to keep yourself busy. There's no point stressing about Stone and Tariq and Eli."

"I suppose you're right, but investigating for a man who thinks he's fallen in love after one date?"

"I know it's never worked out for me,"

Ian said sadly, "but Andrew is different. You'll understand when you meet him."

I opened the door just as Andrew had lifted his hand to knock again.

"I hope I'm not bothering you at a bad time," he said apologetically.

"Not at all. Come in."

Andrew looked to be just under six feet tall. He was lanky, with dark hair that he'd brushed firmly into place, and the side part made him look old-fashioned. He had thick-rimmed glasses, and his skin was pale, as though he didn't get enough sunlight. When I introduced myself and shook his hand, his palm was clammy and sweaty.

"Ian told me that you want to investigate a murder," I said, indicating for Andrew to sit down. "But he hasn't told me the details. Why don't I make us some coffee, and then you can tell me what's going on."

Andrew waited patiently while I took my time making the coffee. I used the distraction to watch him closely. He and Ian chatted about Vegas, and its various attractions, but Andrew said that he was no longer in the mood to vacation.

"I thought this would be the start of me actually relaxing and having some fun," he told Ian. "I thought I'd gotten lucky the very first night. Maybe I did. But I guess I'm just not the kind of person luck sticks to."

Ian said, "I'm not sure luck is a fixed thing. It comes and goes, and you can attract it into your life. It's mostly based on how you're feeling and what kind of work you're doing."

The two fell silent as I approached them again, handing out mugs of steaming coffee.

"Why don't you start at the beginning?" I told Andrew. He seemed like a timid, nervous young man, and Ian was right—he didn't look the type to fall brashly in love with a cocktail waitress. On the other hand, also looked like he had very little experience with women, and maybe he wasn't experienced enough to identify what love was.

Andrew took a deep breath. "It's like this. I work as an accountant in upstate

New York, and the first time I ever met Ian, I told him how I've never been the kind of person to have much fun. I've been working ever since I graduated high school, and I had to pay my way through college. After college, I got a job in an accounting firm, and I've been working hard ever since."

"And you never dated much," I suggested.

Andrew looked at me in surprise. "How did you know? I don't have time for women."

I nodded in understanding. "How did you end up in Vegas?"

"A friend of mine was going to have his bachelor party here. I booked my flights and the stay at the Treasury. But then his wedding got called off, and I thought—I've never been to Vegas and I've already paid for my flights and accommodation, so I might as well come here by myself. So I did."

"When did you get here?"

"Four days ago. The first night, I thought it might've been a mistake to come

A.R. WINTERS

here. I was sitting at the bar, thinking about going straight back home. But then I met Ian, and we chatted a bit, and I thought, maybe Vegas wasn't as unfriendly and dangerous a place as everyone says it is."

"It's not," I said warmly. "I've been living here my whole life, and it's like any other place—there are good bits and bad bits. And if you're a local, you can go to the Strip whenever you want. Prices in Vegas are cheap, and there's lots of fun things to do, and most of the people here are lovely good folk."

"I guess so," Andrew said slowly. "I've never been a people person myself. I'm a numbers guy—numbers are logical in a way people aren't."

"And what did you do after your chat with Ian?"

"I headed over to the slot machines. And then I met a cocktail waitress, Charlene—she told me she'd go out with me if I won the jackpot at one of those special slot machines. She was my lucky charm—as soon as I put my first token into the machine, I won that jackpot."

A cocktail waitress who told a gambler she'd date him if he won a lot of money? That didn't sound to me like a girl looking for real love. "How much was the jackpot?"

"A bit over five hundred thousand."

I raised one eyebrow. "A lot of money."

"I guess. But I was more interested in Charlene—even if I hadn't won that jackpot, I think I'd have convinced her to go out with me."

"Have you been in serious relationships before this?"

Andrew shook his head. "I didn't have time for girls in college, and once I started working—I dated a few women. But everything seemed to end around the three-month mark. Either the women would move on, or they'd start dropping hints about how they want to get married. I wasn't ready to get married then. Of course, things were different with Charlene. I would have married her the next day if she wanted—I could just tell that this was something special."

"And did you go out on that date with Charlene?"

"Yes, her shift ended at five in the morning, and I stayed up to wait for her. Of course, I had to talk to the casino people about cashing in my jackpot, and that took time. They comped my stay, and upgraded me to the penthouse. Isn't that nice of them?"

I smiled politely and Ian said, "They do that for all the big winners."

Andrew nodded. "I can see how it makes sense from a financial perspective. But still, it's a wonderful gesture, and it makes you feel all warm and fuzzy inside."

"So you know logically that it's all about the money, but it still makes you feel happy?"

Andrew's voice grew sheepish. "I guess it's silly."

"Maybe not," I said. "We can't control our emotions."

"Like the way I fell in love with Charlene."

I forced myself not to roll my eyes. Maybe Andrew really had fallen in love with this girl, but so far, I wasn't sure that the feeling had been reciprocal. "Tell me about your date."

"Like I said, her shift ended at five. She took off to get changed, and then we went to the Paris Cat."

"I see." The Paris Cat was a twenty-four-hour jazz bar that served breakfast, dinner, lunch, drinks, and everything in between. Live musicians performed throughout the day, and the views from the window side tables were breathtaking. It was a posh place, and the prices reflected that. "Who picked the place?"

"I asked Charlene for recommendations—she said the Paris Cat would be open, and she wanted some breakfast. She said we could also go to one of the buffets down-stairs, but if we wanted to talk, the Paris Cat would be nice and quiet."

"And you decided to skip the buffets and head to the Paris Cat."

"I wanted to have a chance to talk to her."

"Of course. What did you talk about?"

"I asked her about her job, and what she wanted to do. And she asked me about mine—she was a great listener. She said she grew up in Minnesota, and moved to Vegas three years ago, as soon as she graduated high school. She says she likes working as a waitress, but what she really wants to do is be a kindergarten teacher. She said she loves kids, and thinks they're adorable."

"Do you like kids?"

Andrew shrugged. "I've never thought about kids."

"And what else did you talk about?"

"I told her about my job, and how in my free time I like to renovate houses and rent them out to grow my investment portfolio. She asked me for investment advice, and the kind of things I do, so we talked a bit about that. And then I asked her about her family, and she asked me about mine."

"Right, and how did the date end?"

"Well, I told her I was only in Vegas for a week but now that I'd met her, I was thinking of extending it for another week. And maybe we could go out again for dinner or something. And she said she would love dinner—and the funny thing was, she was actually planning to visit upstate New York in a month's time to visit an old friend of hers."

"What a coincidence. So you made a date for the dinner?"

"The next day was her night off, so we decided to have dinner at nine and I told her I'd look into where I could take her. And then we said goodbye."

"You didn't invite her up to your penthouse suite?"

Andrew blushed like a schoolboy. "No. I would have liked to, but I'm not very good with women, and I was worried she'd say no."

I cynically thought that Charlene would almost certainly have said yes to whatever Andrew had proposed. But maybe I was being too harsh—maybe Charlene would have gone out with Andrew regardless of whether or not he'd won that jackpot.

"So you said goodbye, and you gave her a goodbye kiss?"

Andrew shook his head. "I was—I was a bit nervous. And she didn't move to kiss me, so I just told her I'd see her the next day. I offered to pick her up at her apartment, but she said to text her the name of the restaurant, and she'd go straight there."

"And did you text her?"

"Yes. I decided on Bistro Guillaume. I texted her at five in the afternoon, and she texted back that she was looking forward to it. But then when I showed up at nine, she didn't turn up at all. I waited for two hours, and the bistro even gave me a free glass of wine. When she didn't show up, I called her, but nobody answered her cell phone. I knew she wouldn't have stood me up, so I kept calling her all night. And all through the next day—I kept calling every two or three hours. The next day, at around midday, a man answered, and he told me he was with the police. That Charlene's body had been found, and it was her cell phone. They told me to go into the station, and I did."

Andrew stopped talking, and was silent. The three of us sipped our coffees, and then Andrew finally said, "I couldn't believe it. I mean—she was supposed to be my lucky charm. I never expected such a terrible thing to happen to her. I feel like I'm partly responsible for it."

"How could you be responsible?"

Andrew tilted his head morosely. "The police kept telling me that I would have had nothing to do with it, that I'd just met her. But I feel like our lives were meant to be interwoven. Like it was fate, except something had gone astray."

I lifted one eyebrow. "Do you believe in fate?"

Andrew quickly shook his head. "No, like I said, I'm a logical person. But this whole trip—it's been the complete opposite of what my life is usually like. I won that jackpot because of her. I was going to have a wonderful life with her in it—and now she's not here."

"What did the police tell you?"

Andrew ran a hand through his hair. "They said they couldn't tell me about an open case, and they thanked me for my help. But I kept thinking, there must be something else I can do. So when I met Ian last night, and he told me that he works with you, I decided that I've gotta hire you guys to look into it. I need to find out what happened to Charlene. It's the only thing I can do for someone who was meant to be my lucky charm forever."

"But the police are already looking into it, and they've got resources we don't."

"Cops everywhere are the same," Andrew said, leaning forward, his eyes growing agitated. "They told me Charlene's death was a random act of violence, but I know the statistics! Other than gang violence, most murders are done by people who know the killer. But the cops are already looking to weasel their way out of doing their jobs properly! I need to hire someone who'll do investigate properly, not look for an excuse to stop the investigation. And I know—if Charlene was meant to be my lucky charm, then meeting Ian that first night was just as lucky. I need to hire you guys, and I need to do right by Charlene."

I looked at Andrew in assessment while I took a long sip of my coffee. Andrew sighed deeply and looked off to one side, clearly thinking about Charlene. I could feel Ian staring at me, itching to ask whether I would take the case or not.

I didn't like working on murder cases, and I especially didn't like this one because it was an open investigation, and the police would resent our "interfering." But I actually liked Andrew.

Ian was right: there was something about the guy. He wasn't the sort of person who would normally believe in love at first sight, and he wasn't the kind of person I would imagine trying to hire a PI unless he believed that the probabilities and statistics called for it.

"Okay," I said. "We'll look into what happened. But I can't promise you anything—the police are still looking into things, and I'm sure they'll have better luck than us."

Andrew gazed at me with sad eyes. "Everyone says the police here are swamped, and that they move slowly on things like this. I don't think they'll investigate properly. Did you know ninety percent of murder cases remain unsolved? I can't let Charlene's death be one of those."

There was a hint of truth in Andrew's words. The LVMPD were inundated with all kinds of crime, and they often couldn't be as thorough in their investigations as you'd think they would be. The police in real life were nothing like the police in procedurals like *Law and Order*; in real life, they were bogged down by petty crime, bureaucracy, and all kinds of unexpected delays and political influence.

"I'll grab my PI contract," I told Andrew. "Once we've sorted out the details, I'd like to get straight to work. Starting sooner's always an advantage in these types of investigations. You'll need to tell us everything you've learned so far about Charlene."

Once the contract was signed, and Andrew had paid us a cash advance for the work we'd do, I settled down with my notebook, my pen poised. "Tell me everything you can remember about Charlene," I said. "Every detail, no matter how trivial."

Andrew took my question as an invitation to wax poetic about Charlene's beauty. He'd never seen anyone as gorgeous as her, or as witty, or as funny. I didn't quite believe him, but I kept my silence and nodded my way through his monologue. When he seemed to be done, I asked, "Do you know where Charlene lived?"

Andrew shook his head. "But she worked at the Treasury. I'm sure someone there would know."

I nodded. Andrew was right—all I had to do was ask one of her co-workers, or at the worst, her supervisor, and I'd be able to find out her address. "What about any family or close friends here?"

"I went to her funeral service and met her brother there. His name's Brad, but he didn't want to talk to me. He seemed really broken up about Charlene's death, and I don't know if he'll agree to talk to you."

"Do you have a phone number for him?"

"No. All I know is his name. Brad Nelson."

I wrote the name down thoughtfully. "With any luck, I'll be able to connect the dots and find out enough to go and talk to him. Did you talk to anyone else at the service?"

"Brad was there with a man named Chris, who he introduced as his partner."

"Chris what?"

"I don't know the last name."

"Right. Did you talk to any of Charlene's friends?"

"No. There were a lot of young ladies at the service, I'd guess they were her co-workers at the Treasury. And Charlene mentioned she was living with two room-mates, but I never met them."

"That's okay, you've given us enough to start work. Is there anything else at all that you can tell us about Charlene?"

"Only that she must've been an angel," Andrew said, before launching off into another speech about how wonderful Charlene was.

Ian and I exchanged a glance, but neither of us said anything.

After we assured Andrew that we'd be doing our best to find out what happened to Charlene, and said goodbye to him, Ian turned to me.

"Is that what I sound like whenever I fall for someone?"

I shrugged. "Afraid so. Actually, you're worse."

Ian made a face. "I can't help it. Besides, love makes the world go round."

"And money can't buy happiness, and things happen for a reason."

Ian looked at me and creased his eyebrows together. "Are you making fun of me?"

"No," I said with a sigh. "I just don't know what to say. I don't believe in fate—not really. But this whole thing between Andrew and Charlene, maybe he has a point. Maybe things happen for a reason, and maybe we owe it to him, and to Charlene, to investigate what happened."

Ian nodded. "I wonder who the primary on this case is."

I made a face. "With my luck, it'll be Ryan," I said, referring to my boyfriend, Detective Ryan Dmitriou.

Ryan had been the primary on the last case we'd investigated, and it had been a bit awkward butting heads with him as we interviewed the same suspects over and over again. Ryan didn't approve of private investigators "meddling" in open cases, and I didn't approve of being told not to do my job. Ryan was my first serious boyfriend in a long time, and I didn't want to mess things up.

"Maybe it'll be Elwood," Ian said hopefully.

Detective Elwood was a short, chubby man whom we'd run into on many of our previous investigations—while I'd hated running into him in the past, at this stage, he seemed like a preferable alternative to Ryan.

"We'll have to go to the station and find out what we can about this case at some point," I said. "But in the meantime I should look up everyone on my private investigator's database."

"I'll grab my laptop, and try to find out if there's anything on social media. Oh, and I got this cool new thing," Ian said, pulling what looked like a button from his pocket. "We can use this when we investigate this case."

He handed the button-looking thing over to me, and I turned it around in my hand. It was about half an inch in diameter, and while one side looked like a button, there was something thick and black attached to the other side. "What is it?"

"It's a high-tech recording device," Ian said proudly. "It's tiny, but it's got high-res video and audio capacity."

I looked at the thing in wonder. "It's basically a video camera?"

Ian nodded. "It records everything, and then it transmits all of that to the cloud using the Wi-Fi on my phone. I could record hours and hours of video using this. I'm sure it'll be useful for us."

I couldn't stop gaping. "This must have cost a fortune!"

Ian shrugged modestly. "I've been doing some careful budgeting like my parents keep telling me to. And because I haven't met any interesting, beautiful women these last few weeks, I was able to save up some money and buy it. Plus, I told my lawyer I was going to do a course on coding, and I needed money for that, so he let me have a bit more from my trust fund."

61

I glanced at Ian inquisitively. "But won't he ask you if you learned any coding at all?"

Ian laughed. "The lawyer looks like he's eighty. He's got no idea about coding. I've already taught myself a couple of coding languages for free, using those online coding schools. It's not worth paying to learn coding basics anymore. This nifty camera is much more useful."

Reality settled heavily on my chest. "You know we can't use surreptitious recordings if things go to court."

Ian's eyes crinkled and he nonchalantly tossed his head off to one side. "That's okay. I'm sure this device'll come in handy at some time or the other. Like, let's say we went to talk to the roommate, and she said something, and then we go to talk to the brother. We could play him a recording if we need to."

I wasn't entirely convinced, but I didn't want Ian to regret his purchase. "Maybe. We'll see."

Ian got his laptop, and the next two hours passed in silence. Ian looked up everyone online, Snowflake dozed on top of the fridge, and I traipsed through the labyrinth of my private investigator's database.

At the end of the two hours, we both stopped working, and filled each other in on what we'd found out.

"Charlene Nelson lived just a few miles north of us," I told Ian. "Her two room-mates are Victoria Harris, and Mary Miller. Her brother, Brad Nelson, owns a laundromat in Charleston Heights. His partner is Chris Ellington, and they're business partners—for some reason, I thought they were romantic partners."

"I've seen a lot of pictures of Brad with Chris on social media," Ian said. "I thought for sure they were together. But who knows, maybe they're just very good friends who went into business together? Or maybe they're both business partners *and* romantic partners."

I pressed my lips together thoughtfully. "We'll find out soon enough. The laundromat they own is called Sunset Laundry and the owners are listed as Brad Nelson, Chris Ellington, and the Brad and Chris

Corporation. I looked up Charlene's room-mates. One of them works in retail, and the other works as a waitress. They haven't been in any legal trouble before, and neither has Charlene."

"I looked up Charlene on social media. I saw lots of photos of her at girls' nights out, but nothing of her with men. I'm assuming she was single, and she liked to have the odd night out."

"What about Brad and Chris?"

Ian shrugged "There are a couple of photos of them at a dinner, and they checked into lunch together. Nothing conclusive either way about whether they were business or romantic partners."

"Charlene's been working at the Treasury for the last two years. When she first came to Vegas, she was working as a wait-ress, but she must've gotten her documents in order quickly. She got a job in a Fremont Street casino, before getting into the Treasury. There wasn't anything else particu-larly interesting about her."

"Do you want me to look up the room-mates on social media?"

"No, I'm not sure we'll find anything useful. Most people are careful about their privacy these days, and they try not to share anything incriminating. We'll go have a chat with them, and then if they seem suspect, we can do some more research on them."

"I guess we're heading off to the police station now?"

I sighed. "We may as well. And who knows, maybe you're right—maybe this is Elwood's case."

"At least we'll learn more about how she was killed," Ian said, "It's the first step toward finding out who the killer is. Who would want to kill a cocktail waitress?"

CHAPTER 4

*I*an and I were just about to put away our computers and get ready to head over to the precinct when there was a loud, urgent knock on my door.

We exchanged a glance, wordlessly wondering who it might be this time.

"Maybe it's Nanna," Ian suggested.

But something in the urgency of that knock had me worried, and I rushed over to the door and flung it open.

"Stone!"

My heart soared, and my eyes widened.

This was the first time I'd seen Stone in broad daylight; since those two dark-suited men had shown up, I'd only ever run into Stone under cover of the night. And those times, he'd been dressed in all black, all the better to blend into the background.

Before Stone had gone undercover, his usual uniform had been dark jeans, dress shoes, and a crisp white shirt. Today, he was wearing Bermuda shorts, a loud-print Hawaiian shirt, and a baseball cap. His dark eyes glimmered from under the cap, and I felt myself warmed by the strength of his presence. It was almost like things had gone back to normal—other than that horrible shirt, which I would never have imagined him wearing.

I stepped aside, and Stone walked in.

"Thanks for the text," Stone said. "I'm looking forward to seeing him."

"You mean Tariq?" Ian said. He was grinning, his face lit up with delight at seeing Stone again. "I'll go get him! But I haven't seen you in ages—it's good to know you've been safe, man."

Stone and Ian did a strange handshake-fist-pump thing, and then Stone turned to look at me. I was hovering near the closed door, wondering what to do.

Before I could say anything, there was

another knock on the door, this one quieter and less rushed.

I opened it to let Tariq inside.

Stone and Tariq stared at each other for a few long seconds.

Finally, Tariq smiled, and they embraced in a manly hug. When they pulled apart and looked at each other, the similarities between the two men were glaringly obvious—they were both tall, both handsome in their own ways, and both men of few words.

Stone said, "Everything good?"

Tariq nodded somberly. "Here in one piece. You?"

Stone grimaced. "Surviving. You got all the details from Johnson?"

"Yes. We are on track?"

"Everything's going smoothly. I'll let you know once all the arrangements are made for the trip to DC."

"I will go back to Ian's apartment now," Tariq said. "I have to get used to laying low again."

And with that, he disappeared.

Stone stared after the man, even after

the door to my apartment was closed shut.

I was suddenly nervous.

This was it! This was Stone's only way to clear his name, and I didn't want anything to go wrong.

I wanted him to be safe, I wanted him to be able to come out of hiding, and I wanted everything to go back to normal. But something about Stone's pensiveness, the lack of his usual lightheartedness, made me unsure.

"I'm glad you and Tariq met each other again," I said uncertainly, hoping that Stone would volunteer some information about their plans.

But Stone only looked at me, and a corner of his mouth twitched upwards, as though he knew I was fishing for information.

"You need to be careful," Stone said. "I know for a fact that Eli has wind of Tariq's presence. He doesn't know the man's staying with Ian though, and with any luck he'll never find out."

Stone's words sent a shiver down my spine. I'd met Eli once, and given what I'd learned of his past, I knew that the man was ruthless, and dangerous. "I'll be careful."

"You're not working on any cases now, are you?"

Ian and I exchanged a glance. Even Ian could sense the danger that we were in, and for once, Ian didn't seem all that excited about our upcoming investigation.

I took a deep breath, and looked into Stone's dark, jet black eyes. "We've just accepted a murder investigation. A cocktail waitress, Charlene Nelson, was killed a few days back."

Stone nodded, and watched me steadily. I could see the concern in his eyes, and I fully expected him to tell me to drop the case.

"I read about it in the papers," Stone said. "Bad business."

I shifted from one foot to another. "I'm sure it'll be fine."

This time, Stone's eyes danced with amusement. "When has a murder investigation ever not turned dangerous for you?"

I couldn't help smiling. "It's part of the job, I guess."

"And I'll be right here to help her," Ian chimed in enthusiastically. "We're going to stick together."

Stone turned to look at Ian, and nodded seriously. "You do that." And then he turned back to me. "You need to wrap up this case quickly. I'll help you as much as I can."

Gratitude surged through my veins, and I smiled at him.

All over again, I remembered why Stone and I had become such good friends, and why I'd found myself falling for him. You couldn't help but like a man who supported you as much as he could. Stone didn't like me getting into dangerous situations, but his response to that was to force me to take Krav Maga classes and learn how to shoot a gun. He never discouraged me from accepting clients, or told me that I'd be better off pursuing a career at the casino.

"You don't have to," I said. "You're already in trouble. I want you to stay safe and get this whole thing sorted out."

Stone's eyes locked on to mine. "I'm always safe," he said softly. "I don't want you worrying about me."

He took a few steps forward, and gave me a quick hug. For a few seconds, I leaned against Stone's broad chest, and savored the warmth of his strong arms wrapped around me. I couldn't help but worry about him, but his presence always made me feel so safe and protected.

Before I knew it, Stone had stepped back, and he ran one finger lightly along my jaw. Sparks danced wherever his skin touched mine.

"I'll keep an eye on you," he said seriously. "Everything will be fine."

He walked out the door, and out of view, but I believed him.

Everything would be fine.

CHAPTER 5

*J*an and I couldn't help but feel slightly nervous as we headed over to the precinct.

It was almost lunchtime, and the Vegas sun blazed down as we drove over slowly. I checked my rearview mirror every few seconds, trying to see if there was a car tailing me—but I couldn't see anyone.

"I feel like we should stop this investigation into Charlene's death," Ian said, sounding as nervous as I felt.

"No, what you said earlier was right—focusing on a case will help keep us busy. And it'll make us look like we're leading normal lives. If Eli or his men decide to tail us, they'll see that we're busy with work—

not sitting around at home all day doing nothing."

"Speaking of sitting around, do you think Tariq really will be safe in my apartment?"

I nodded rapidly as I parked the car. "I'm sure nobody saw him come in, and he won't be going out or speaking with anyone. And your apartment is safer than mine. Eli doesn't even know that you and Stone are friends."

We were still thinking about Stone and Tariq as we headed into the precinct, and said hello to the desk sergeant.

"We're here to see Detective Elwood," I said hopefully. "He's not expecting us, but I'm sure he'll agree to talk to us."

Ian and I made our way over to the open space work area where the detectives sat around at their desks, and worked on their various cases.

Detective Elwood was a short, balding man with a perpetual scowl. We found him at his desk hunched over piles of paper-work, a mug of milky coffee in front of him.

There was a time when the sight of us would make his scowl deepen, but today, when he looked up at Ian and I, a spark of hopefulness glittered in his watery gray eyes.

"Did you two stop by to give me more cupcakes?"

Ian and I glanced at each other sheepishly, and shrugged. The last few times, we'd brought some cupcakes over for Elwood—not that they were bribes or anything, but they seemed to put him in a better mood.

"Not today," Ian said. "But I found this amazing recipe for red velvet cupcakes— actually, they're red velvet surprise cupcakes because there's a little surprise in each of them. They're going to be absolutely delicious!"

Elwood looked at me and Ian warily as we pulled out two chairs and sat down opposite him. "And when are you going to be making these cupcakes?"

"Tomorrow," Ian promised. "Well, I was going to make them tomorrow. But then I met this guy, and he wants us to investigate something. So I'm going to make them as soon as I finish my investigation."

Elwood leaned back in his chair. "And let me guess, you want me to help in your investigation. So when your investigation finishes quicker, you'll be giving me those —what did you call them?—red velvet surprise cupcakes—sooner."

Ian beamed at Elwood unashamedly. "Exactly! Ever since I learned how to bake, I'm really interested in baking more cupcakes. It's so much fun, and it's always nice to eat them after you're done with the baking. And, of course, share them with people you admire—like you."

Elwood's brow cleared, and he smiled happily. "I would say you're trying to bribe me, but I did love those hazelnut cupcakes you brought for me the other day. I definitely can't wait to try these red velvet surprise cupcakes of yours."

"I'm glad you feel that way," I said quickly. "We really would appreciate your help. You've been on the force for so long, and you always have great ideas when it comes to cases."

That last statement wasn't accurate, but I'd decided a bit of flattery might help our cause.

Elwood glanced at me suspiciously, as though he was trying to guess whether I was being sarcastic or not, but my face gave nothing away. He said, "What case do you want info on?"

"Charlene Nelson. She was killed a few days back."

Elwood pressed his lips together, and shook his head unhappily. "That's an open case. And it's not mine."

"But I'm sure you can tell us a few things. Whose case is it?"

Elwood raised one bushy eyebrow at me. "That boyfriend of yours."

My eyes widened. "Ryan?"

Elwood looked at me smugly and winked. "I would've thought he'd tell you himself. Unless he doesn't know you're investigating this one?"

My brows knit together, and my stomach did strange, nauseating flip-flops. Not again!

The last time Ryan and I had worked

together on the same case, it had been downright uncomfortable. Ryan hadn't wanted me "influencing" witnesses or suspects, and I hadn't thought our investigation could hurt the cops'. After all, there was no law against talking to a few people.

I sat there in silence for a few seconds, trying to process my feelings. Since Ryan and I had already worked together once, and worked out a few kinks, we'd hopefully do better the second time around.

When I didn't say anything, Ian said, "Maybe you could tell us what you're allowed to tell the public, and then we can go talk to Ryan. Where is he now?"

"Out on a case," Elwood grumbled. "But he should be back soon. Why don't you just wait for him to get back?"

Ian shrugged. His nights at the casinos had taught him some basic bluffing skills. "Sure, but it would be nice if you could help us—that way, I can get started on those red velvet surprise cupcakes sooner."

Elwood grumbled under his breath, and slowly pushed himself out of his chair. He waddled away from us, presumably heading toward the room where files for open investigations were kept. We waited a few minutes, 'til he returned, carrying a single piece of paper.

My heart fell. I'd been hoping to see him carrying a large, thick file—presumably one that would have all the details of the case.

"This is what I can tell the public," Elwood said, looking down at the paper. "Charlene Nelson's body was found off the highway in the desert, three days back. The LVMPD are investigating the case, and are not able to comment further at this time." Elwood looked up from the paper and grinned at us. "So that's all I can tell the public."

I tilted my head backward, and stifled a groan.

"I'm sure you can tell us something more," Ian said pleadingly.

Elwood glanced around, as though he was wary of being watched. But by now, most of the cops at the precinct knew me and Ian, and they surely wouldn't be too suspicious of Elwood talking to us.

"Maybe I'll see what I can do," Elwood

said slowly. "There might be some files I could show you."

"What files?" said a familiar voice.

Detective Ryan Dimitriou took a few brisk steps forward. He seemed to materialize out of thin air, standing next to Elwood, and grinning down at us.

He was as handsome as ever, with his sparkling gray eyes, tan skin, and broad shoulders. As usual, I smiled back at him, and little pitter patter footsteps ran across my heart.

"We're investigating a case that's yours," I said. I tried my best not to sound apologetic—there was no reason to apologize. Yet. "Charlene Nelson."

A hint of dismay flashed in Ryan's eyes before he turned quickly to look at Elwood.

Elwood raised his eyebrows at Ryan, and said, "I've been telling them what we've told the press. No more than that." He held out the paper to Ryan, as though it were proof of his innocence.

"We were hoping you could tell us a bit more," Ian said.

Ryan looked at us and sighed. "Come

on, let's go head over to a conference room and chat."

We followed Ryan over to one of the small conference rooms on the right of the bullpen. It looked different from when I'd last been here—instead of a plain wooden table surrounded by metal chairs, there were a few loveseats scattered around, and a comfy-looking wingback armchair covered in a light floral pattern. The room looked warm and cozy, and I gave Ryan a quizzical look. "Did someone here take an interior decorating course?"

Ryan shrugged. "We're supposed to be friendlier. A lot of the people who come in have gone through trauma, and want to report a crime. This room is meant to make them feel at ease. I'll be right back with the Charlene Nelson file."

Ian and I settled in and waited, our nerves slightly on edge. A few minutes later, Ryan appeared, brandishing a thick file.

"What did you want to know?" he said, settling in on the loveseat opposite us.

"Anything you can tell us," I said hopefully. "I know it's still an open investigation, but Ian and I have to do our best. So I'll leave it up to you—let us know anything you think might help us."

Ryan's cheeks dimpled. "I'll see what I can do. You know I'm not supposed to be telling you any of this at all right? We never had this conversation."

Ian and I nodded like bobbleheads.

"I really appreciate you helping us out," I said warmly. "I know it's... I know you don't like us investigating open cases. But we'll do what we can to stay out of your way."

"It's a slow investigation anyway," Ryan said, leaning back in his chair. "We're flooded with all kinds of touristy crime. We need to keep the tourists happy, so the mayor wants us to focus on creating a safe city for them, make the Strip safer, all that kind of stuff."

I leaned forward. "What have you got?"

"I can show you photos of the scene," Ryan said, pulling out the crime scene photos he'd been talking about and handing them over to us. "Charlene's body was found in the desert off the highway, but she'd been stabbed. Whoever killed her did it somewhere else and then transported her body to the desert. The blood stains found weren't consistent with her being killed in the desert."

"You think they were trying to hide the body?"

"I do. It would never have been found, except for one of those hipster amateur photographers who decided to go to strange places to take artistic shots. He's the one who found the body."

A shudder racked my body. "How terrible. Lucky about the photographer, though. If he hadn't been there, the body might've lain in the desert for ages."

The photos were gory, and I glanced at them quickly before handing them over to Ian. They showed a young girl who had freckled skin and blond hair with dark roots showing. Her skin had gone a strange shade of white, and her eyes were vacant and unseeing. She was wearing a silver necklace with a heart-shaped locket, and a T-shirt and Bermuda shorts. Her clothes were covered in blood, and her limbs seemed to be at odd angles.

"Do you know when she was killed? Andrew told us he was supposed to see her at nine at night for their dinner date, so she must've been killed before then."

"One of the neighbors last saw her at seven. She'd gone out for a walk."

"So she must've been killed between seven and nine," I mused thoughtfully.

When we handed the photos back, Ryan asked, "Who hired you? Brad, her brother, right?" Ian and I exchanged a look, but neither of us said anything, so Ryan went on. "Brad was really shook up each time we went to talk to him. He'd been having dinner with his partner Chris the night Charlene was killed, and he was so upset when we talked to him. I think he and Charlene had been really close, growing up together, and then moving to Vegas together. I hate cases like this, and I had to tell Brad he'd probably do well with some counseling."

I shifted in my seat, not looking forward to speaking with Brad. "No, it was actually

Andrew, the man who'd gone out on a date with Charlene just before she was killed."

"Right. I remember him. He kept saying this might be his fault somehow, that maybe it was all fate. You know, you meet people like that sometimes—they come to Vegas, and something strange happens, and they think it's all because of fate, or luck."

"We do play up the Lady Luck aspect of life."

Ryan's gray eyes grew thoughtful, and he looked off into the distance. "Not everything is about luck."

"But some things are," I argued. "Like running into you in that parking lot. We might not have met if it hadn't been for that day."

Ryan smiled at me. "We might still have met. If you do believe in fate, something important that's meant to happen will happen anyway. But you don't believe in fate, do you?"

"Not always. Before I started working as an investigator, I didn't believe in fate at all. But now—I'm not so sure."

"Did you talk to the roommates?" Ian

said impatiently, noticing how our conversation had strayed away from the case.

Ryan nodded. "I did. We talked everyone, but no one seemed to have any motive for killing her. We think this might just be a random one-off crime, but we're still investigating, of course."

"Did you learn anything unusual?" Ryan shook his head, and closed the folder. "No, it all seemed very normal."

We sat in silence for a few seconds, and then I said, "Is that all you can tell us?"

"Yep." A serious look had come over Ryan's face, a look that I'd come to know as his "cop face." "I'm afraid that's it. I should've asked you who hired you first. I'd just assumed that Brad, the brother, had hired you. But now that I know it's not him, I have to tell you guys to be careful. I don't want you upsetting any of the people who knew Charlene. Especially not Brad. He seems so fragile."

"You know we're always professional." I

tried not to sound defensive, but I could feel that old annoyance bubbling up.

Ryan leaned forward and smiled into my eyes. "I know. You're a good detective. But I remember Brad too well—it's hard to deliver bad news to loved ones. He kept mumbling that it was his fault, that he should've been a better brother. He needs counseling sooner rather than later, not some nosy PI—don't glare, you know you're nosy!—poking around."

I sighed. "Oh, all right. We'll be less nosy. And super discreet. We always are."

"So you keep telling me," Ryan said, with a twinkle in his eyes. "But I wouldn't be doing my job right if I didn't tell you not to meddle too much. And you do know that you have to stick to the rules, and you can't break into people's places, or steal their mail, or go through their trash, or record them without their knowledge—all the things like that."

I tried my best to keep a straight face, but out of the corner of my eye I could see Ian fidgeting and looking away guiltily. He'd left his tiny button-sized camera in the car, and hopefully no one else would find out about it.

"We know all of that," I said. I tried my best not to sound as sheepish as I felt.

"On previous cases, some suspects have accused you of breaking into their apartments. I heard you once even took Nanna with you."

"That's not—" I wanted to say that it wasn't true, but it actually was.

Ryan stared at me seriously. "I don't want you to compromise an open investigation, especially one that I'm working on. You got lucky a few times in the past, but you can't keep breaking the rules."

Our conversation had started out so nicely. "I thought we'd be working together on this one."

Ryan rubbed his temples as though I was giving him a headache. "We can work together. I just don't want you making people feel uncomfortable. I feel so sorry for the poor brother."

"And you can't feel sorry for anyone else who wants to know the truth?"

"Maybe."

"Well, our client wants us to investigate and find out that truth."

"He didn't even know her properly. He's just someone who's decided to believe in fate and lucky charms and things that are meant to be. I think he's one of those people who's come into lots of money suddenly, and doesn't know how to spend it."

"He's an accountant," Ian protested. "He knows perfectly well, better than most people, how to track his spending and income."

"It's always the quiet, logical ones who become obsessed and dangerous," Ryan said. "I know I can't discourage you from looking into this case, but I do have to do my job and tell you not to obstruct the police investigation. Don't let your meddling make our job harder. *We're* the professionals."

I glowered at Ryan silently. I was a professional too, just as much as him.

Charlene's death was a mystery I was determined to investigate properly, and with any luck, I'd be the one to solve it.

CHAPTER 6

*I*an and I went straight from the precinct to my parents' house in North Las Vegas. Before Ian and I had accepted this case, I'd agreed to a family lunch today, and there was no backing out of this.

I didn't like being told how to do my job, and I wished I could take a bit of a break from seeing Ryan so frequently. I was hopeful that our relationship would get back to the happy, calm normalcy that we'd enjoyed, as soon as this case was over. But while we were working on it, I didn't feel like explaining myself or my methods to Ryan.

Ian and I pulled up in front of my

parents' house, and got out of the car warily. We both put on fake grins when Nanna opened the door, and we followed her into the den where everyone else, other than Ryan, was already gathered around.

There was Wes, Nanna's new husband, and Wes's brother Glenn, who also happened to be my downstairs neighbor and a retired baker, and Glenn's aging hippie girlfriend Karma. For once, my mother was also settled down in a chair, and not rushing around in the kitchen, and my dad sat next to her. They were all talking animatedly about the upcoming baseball season, and whether the Mets would do well or not. I didn't follow baseball, so I lost interest when the talk turned to batting averages and previous injuries.

"Is Ryan coming?" my mother asked me, and I nodded.

"He should be here in a few minutes. We've just met him at the station."

My mother smiled, and watched me carefully. "That sounds nice. But was it for work?"

I grimaced and sighed. "Yes, we have to

investigate another case that Ryan is working on."

The baseball talk died down abruptly, and everyone stared at me.

"You two worked together on that reality TV show murder, didn't you?" Nanna said gently. "That worked out okay in the end."

"Yeah, I think we'll soon start getting used to working with each other." I tried to sound upbeat and hopeful, but the emotions I wanted to project didn't quite make it into my voice.

"I'm sure everything will be fine," Wes said reassuringly. "Every relationship has its hiccups. Because you and Ryan work in the same business, your hiccups are a bit different from most people's, that's all."

I glanced at Karma. Glenn's girlfriend frequently had "premonitions" that I used to discount—but the last few premonitions she'd had turned out to be true. I was hoping she would say something about my relationship with Ryan, but instead, she glanced off to one side, and refused to meet my eyes.

I wasn't going to let her get off that easily, so I said, "Karma, you don't have some kind of premonition about this, do you?"

Karma finally turned to look at me and smiled. She had make-up free, wrinkled skin, and straight gray hair that fell to her waist. As usual, she was wearing a black tank top, and a long, flowing bohemian skirt.

"I don't have a premonition," she said. "But relationships can be tricky. I'm sure everything will work out for the best. What happened to that other nice young man who used to come to family lunches, Stone? The one you kept saying was just a friend?"

Nanna burst out laughing. "I don't see how Tiffany can stay 'just friends' with a man who's so nice and handsome. We never do see him around these days."

"I heard he was wanted by the CIA," my mother said, thin-lipped.

"It's all a misunderstanding," I reassured her. "It'll get sorted out soon."

Ian and I exchanged a glance. I wished I

could tell my parents the truth about Stone, but it was still too soon.

My mother made a tut-tut noise. "No matter how good looking or polite someone is, it's best to stay away from them if they keep getting into danger."

Ian said, "Tiffany keeps getting into danger."

But that just made my mother shake her head. "Too often for my liking."

I smiled to myself, glad that I rarely told my mother how dangerous my work was— I tried not to let her know that I'd been stalked and shot at.

"Why can't you focus on your work at the casino?" Mom went on. "I heard from my friend Ruby's sister Carla, that you'd been offered a job as a pit boss, or to get fast-tracked to management."

I rolled my eyes. "The Vegas gossip mill is still in session."

"But it's true, isn't it?" my mother insisted. "Why turn down a nice management position?"

"Because I could never work in management after working on the floor," I said honestly. "After the Treasury brought in those new executives and tried to cut costs, I saw firsthand how out of touch management is with the people who do the real work on the floor. It's all theory to management—but when you're on the ground, doing your job, you have to be practical. I don't want to be one of those people who make up ridiculous rules and targets, and tries to force them on everyone else."

"Not all management is bad," Wes said. "I know someone—"

The conversation was interrupted by a loud knock at the door, and my mother stood up and smiled at me. "That must be Ryan. I'm sure it'll be nice for you two to have a good family meal together. Stop thinking about work all the time, and maybe focus on each other."

With that, she was gone. Ryan followed her in a few seconds later, and I noticed that my mother was holding a large bunch of flowers.

"Ryan brought these over," she said. "Isn't that nice of him?"

Ryan and I exchanged a smile. He

must've stopped off at the florist's, and I was actually glad to see him again, away from work.

Greetings were exchanged all around, and then Ryan said. "What are we talking about?"

There was silence for a few seconds, and then Ian quickly said, "Baseball. Do you think Kris Bryant's going to have another good season?"

Ryan looked as though he didn't believe that we'd really been talking about baseball, but everyone started talking about the Red Sox, and what their odds were this time round.

A few minutes later, my mother announced that the roast was ready, and we all headed over to the dining room, where we settled down for a delicious meal of Greek-style lamb, roast potatoes, and Greek salad. It just so happened that Ryan and I were sitting at different ends of the table, and for once, we barely spoke to each other throughout the meal. It was as though everyone at the table was intent on keeping the conversation to non-offensive topics, but I couldn't help feeling the slight awkwardness and tension every now and then.

Ryan got a text halfway through the meal, and just before dessert was served, he excused himself and said he had an emergency. He gave me a quick peck on the cheek, and then he was gone.

After he'd left, and dessert was served, my mother turned to me and said, "Things will never work out between you two unless you're honest about what's happening. I know it's difficult to work together, but you can't hide things from him."

"He said he'd found out we'd broken into a suspect's house with Nanna once," I said slowly. "We can't be honest about things like that."

"Then maybe you should stop breaking into suspect's houses."

I looked at my mother and shook my head. "That break-in hadn't been my idea. It's always Nanna and Ian who come up with crazy plans like that."

"And you go along with it! So at some

level, you must think it's a good idea after all."

My mother had a point.

But I didn't want to think about investigations and relationships anymore. Instead, I bit into the delicious berry cheesecake that my mother had made for dessert. It was cool, creamy, and sweet with the perfect amount of berry tanginess—just what I needed to take my mind off things.

Even if it was only for a brief moment or two.

CHAPTER 7

*A*fter lunch was over, Glenn and Karma invited Wes and Nanna to come over to their apartment for coffee.

"We'd love to," Nanna said. "Maybe Tiffany can give us a ride, and tell us more about her case."

Ian and I exchanged a glance—Nanna was always curious about my cases, and very often, she insisted on "helping out."

But it wouldn't be a bad idea to tell someone else what we'd learned so far. Maybe discussing the events would help us get some idea as to who the main suspect should be. So as I drove back to my place, Ian and I told Nanna and Wes everything we'd learned from the police and from our chat with Andrew.

"Let me get this straight," Nanna said, after we told her what we knew, "Charlene went out for a walk at seven, and was seen by one of her neighbors leaving. She didn't show up for the date at 9 o'clock. So she must've been killed sometime between then."

"Exactly," Ian said. "But nobody remembers seeing her. I know that neighborhood, and it's full of cheap apartments. People move in and out, and nobody knows their neighbors, or even pays attention to what's going on. Folks don't really look around much when they're in a hurry to get to where they're going, and when they've been told to respect everyone else's privacy. For all we know, someone might have pulled a gun on Charlene and kidnapped her, and no one would have noticed."

"And that's what the police think happened?"

"I guess," Ian said. "They don't think it's anyone related to her. It's hard to investigate a crime when the criminal is some random psychopath."

"That might just be what happened to Charlene, though," I admitted reluctantly, as I drove toward my apartment. "As far as we know, anyone could have killed Charlene—even someone who never knew her."

"I don't buy that for a second," Nanna declared staunchly. "Pretty much every single murder is committed by someone who knew the victim. Just because it's Vegas doesn't mean the statistics have changed."

There was silence for a few minutes, as we all thought about that, and I pulled up at my apartment and parked. As we headed upstairs, Nanna said to Wes, "I think I'll go with Tiffany and Ian and chat a bit more about the case."

Wes looked at me and gave me an apologetic smile. "I know you don't like your Nanna getting involved in your investigations. But she won't listen to me when I say not to."

"Just because I'm old," Nanna said, "doesn't mean I can't be useful. I've got enough brains and wit to help Tiffany with her investigations. And I'm not even that old. Tiff might've been doing this for a while now, but an extra set of ears to hear all the details never hurts."

"As long as that's all you're planning on doing—listening," I said to Nanna. "We're happy to talk to you about it."

I turned to Wes. "Would you like to come up to my apartment for a bit as well?"

Wes shook his head. "I don't mean to be rude, but thinking about things like murders gives me the creeps. I'd rather go and help Glenn with his baking. He said something about Danishes."

We got into the elevator, and said goodbye to Wes when he got off at Glenn's floor. And then, Nanna, Ian and I headed over to my apartment and settled down to rehash the case.

"The odd thing here," Nanna said, "is that Charlene didn't have a boyfriend. Usually, it's the spouse or the boyfriend that's the main suspect."

I nodded. "That's one of the things that makes the cops think it was a random killing. I mean, she did meet Andrew and agree to go out with him, but he's our client."

"You suspected clients in the past," Nanna said. "Don't you think Andrew might have had something to do with Charlene's death? Maybe she insulted him, or turned him down, and he's not telling you the truth. Maybe he killed her, and now he's panicking and hiring you two to dig up dirt on everyone else, just so he can protect himself."

I shook my head. "I know something similar's happened on a previous case, but I don't think that's what's going on with Andrew. And I don't think the cops suspect him either."

"I agree," said Ian. "Andrew doesn't seem like a potential killer to me. For one, he seemed genuinely upset by Charlene's death—he has this whole belief about luck and destiny now."

"But he might be making all that up," Nanna said.

I got up to make us each a mug of coffee, and said, "I don't think so. Even if he was making all that up, I'm sure he's got a solid alibi. He must've been in the casino until eight thirty or so, and then after that, he was sitting in the restaurant waiting for Charlene to show up. Besides, if he was any kind of suspect at all, Ryan would have told me, and warned me off taking the case."

Nanna looked at me shrewdly as I returned to the living room with the coffee. "Has Ryan warned you off the case at all?"

I shrugged, and sipped my coffee. "Not in so many words, but he's not happy about it."

"You can't be with a man who doesn't support you," Nanna said. "We each have something we're meant to do on this earth, and your life partner needs to support your work. Doesn't mean they have to be super enthusiastic, or actually physically help you out, but they need to be there with you in spirit. Seems to me that Ryan will never be there with you in spirit."

I sighed. "I really like him, and he's great and always so calm and drama-free. Being with him is like relaxing next to a quiet stream. Maybe he'll come around in time—

he's never had problems with my being a private investigator before."

"That was before we worked on the same case as him," Ian reminded me. "He wasn't happy about that."

"He wasn't too bad today. I mean, he showed us the crime scene photos and told us a bit about the case before warning us to not to comprise his investigation."

"And there'll be other cases where he won't want you to 'compromise his investigation.' Any more of these run-ins and he'll soon be warning you not to investigate at all. "

I frowned and leaned forward. "No, no. I've made it clear that I'm a private investigator, and I like being one. Looking into all these mysteries lets me help people. I don't mind working as a dealer, but I'm not making people's lives better when I hand out blackjack cards. But I can find things out for people, and I can help them out— I'm not about to stop being a PI."

Nanna nodded seriously. "I don't think you should stop. I mean, I haven't been playing poker much these days, but that's not because Wes doesn't like me to, or anything like that. He knows about my poker playing, and he doesn't mind—I've just cut down on playing because I'm busy with other things. You could stop being a private investigator sometime in the future, if you get busy with other things—but you should never change who you are just to make a man happy."

"How come you tell Tiffany not to change, but everyone keeps telling me I need to change if I'm going to find a long-term girlfriend?" Ian said.

Nanna and I looked at each other and grinned. Ian's tragic love life was legendary —from women dumping him as soon as they discovered they couldn't get their hands on his trust fund, to girlfriends stalking him and trying to strong-arm him into marriage.

"That's because people keep taking advantage of you," Nanna told him. "You don't need to change in order to find a girl-friend—you need to change so that people stop taking advantage of your kindness."

Ian took a thoughtful sip of his coffee,

and I said, "But back to Charlene's death. She didn't have a boyfriend, and Andrew isn't a suspect."

"Maybe she had a secret boyfriend," Nanna suggested. "Maybe nobody knew about him, but he's the one who killed her."

I wrote down "secret boyfriend?" in my notebook, and chewed my lip thoughtfully. "I'll try to see if anyone could know about it —maybe the roommates would have some inkling. If Charlene went out on dates, or brought a guy over, they're the ones who would know."

"Maybe it's not love," Ian said. "Tiff, you keep saying that it's either love or money that gets people killed. Maybe in Charlene's case, it was money."

"It doesn't sound to me like Charlene had money," I said. "I know Andrew was very taken with her, but she sounds like the kind of woman who would go out with a man only if he had money—she went out with Andrew just because he won that jack-pot. If Charlene insisted on limiting her dating pool to men with money, then she couldn't have had much wealth herself."

"I think you're right," Nanna said slowly. "I don't think Charlene had any money worth getting killed over. But if she didn't have any love interests, maybe her family should be the next suspects."

"Andrew said that Charlene had a brother here," Ian told than Nanna. "We've already looked up his details on the database and the Internet, but Andrew said the brother seemed really upset by Charlene's death. He tried to talk to Brad—that's Charlene's brother—at the funeral, but he was too upset to talk much."

"But you and Tiffany still need to talk to him," Nanna said, regarding us with thoughtful eyes. "Brad must've already talked to the police—do you know if they've learned anything useful from him?"

"I don't think he said anything particularly helpful," I said. "If he had, I'd like to think that Ryan would have mentioned it to me."

"But if Brad didn't want to talk to people at the funeral," Ian said, "he probably won't want to talk to us. Lots of people don't like talking to private investigators, and if he's not talking to Charlene's friends, Brad's definitely not going to want to talk to an investigator."

"You just need to go in disguise," Nanna said brightly. "Act like you're selling Girl Scout cookies or something like that."

"We're a little too old to look like we're selling cookies," I said doubtfully, "but maybe you've got an idea. Ian and I should pretend to be interviewing Brad for something else."

"Where does Brad live?" Nanna said.

I looked up my notes, where I'd written down all of Brad's details. I'd already told Nanna that Brad owned a laundromat with his partner Chris, and I wasn't sure if he'd be home or at the laundromat now.

"He's more likely to be at the laundromat now," Ian said, "maybe we should just drive up and try to talk to him there."

"Why don't we call him at home," I said, "and see where he is?"

"You could just do the whole interview over the phone," Nanna said. "I know you don't like talking to people over the phone, but it's easier to keep up an act if you're on the phone—and if Brad has something to hide, we can follow up with him in person."

I thought about the idea for a few seconds, and then admitted that Nanna was probably right. "Let's give him a call, and see what he has to say."

"I know what we should say," Ian said, "people love to be on TV—we'll just pretend we're doing a TV show."

I wasn't sure about that—Ian had gone through a period of having reality TV show fever, but I handed him my phone, along with my notebook with Brad's details. Ian put my cell phone on speaker, and dialed Brad's home number. It rang about four times, and then finally, a male voice answered.

"Is this Brad Nelson?" Ian said, and Brad answered that yes, it was him.

"This is Jeremy Whitkins," Ian said. "I'm a TV show producer, and I'm planning an exciting new show about laundromats. I wonder if I could ask you a few questions, for research purposes? I'd be happy to give you a credit on the show, when it goes live."

"No thank you," Brad said instantly. "I can't help out with that."

"It'll just take a few minutes of your time," Ian pleaded. "We'd really appreciate it."

"I'm sure there are other laundromat owners who'd be happy to talk to you," Brad said. "I'm going through some things in my personal life, and I'd rather not talk to too many people now."

And then, the line went dead.

"He hung up on us!" Ian looked at me in shock. "He wasn't even impressed when I said that I was from TV!"

I made a face. "I'm only surprised that he was so harsh. He must really be grieving."

"Maybe he just doesn't like TV," Nanna said. "I know it's hard to believe, but some people don't watch TV at all."

"I never watched TV until I met Ian," I said. "Who has time for that? I'd rather read a good book if I've got a moment free."

"Maybe you need to try something else," Nanna suggested. "Some other way to get him to talk."

I had a flash of inspiration, and I redialed Brad's number, and put the phone on speaker.

When he answered, I verified that I was talking to Brad, and then I said, "Congratulations! I'm calling from Anderson's Grocery, and I wanted to let you know that you're in the running to win a ten thousand dollar check as a thank you for shopping at our stores."

It had been a wild guess on my part that Brad shopped at Anderson's—but I assumed, that like many people who lived in Vegas, he must've visited their stores at least once in the last year. And even if he hadn't, who would turn down free money?

"Really?" Brad sounded wary.

"Absolutely!" I tried to muster up as much enthusiasm as I could. "All you need to do to win the money is answer a few quick questions about your experience shopping in our stores."

"The last time I went was over a month ago," Brad said slowly.

"That's fine," I said. "We're looking for all kinds of opinions. Now, the first question is, did you shop for yourself, or do you have any family in Las Vegas?"

The phone went silent for a few seconds, and then Brad said, in a slightly choked voice, "I'm sorry, I can't do this."

Once again, the line went dead.

Ian, Nanna and I all stared at each other incredulously.

"I can't believe he did that!" Ian said again. "Who turns down free money?"

"Maybe he really is in shock over his sister's death," Nanna said. "That question about whether he had any family in Vegas —that must've been what upset him. He sounded so upset."

"I know," I said, still not quite believing that he'd hung up on me and turned down the free money. "But it's been a few days since Charlene died, and you'd think that anyone would be happy to answer a few questions about their shopping habits to get ten thousand dollars."

"Maybe he's an introvert," Ian said. "Some people are hermits, and they're phobic about talking to other people."

Nanna suddenly grinned, and her eyes

sparkled with life. "I know what to do! Hand me the phone."

She redialed Brad's number, and put the phone on speaker.

This time, when Brad answered after a few rings, Nanna made sure of who she was talking to, and then she said, "My name's Gwenda Larsen, and I'm calling from the Las Vegas Police Department. I know you've talked to one of our officers recently, and I want to clarify some of the things that you talked about."

Brad was saying something like, "Sure, I'd be happy to do that," but I was instantly on my feet, waving my arms in the air, trying to signal Nanna to hang up.

"Let me just put you on hold for a minute," Nanna said, and then she pressed the hold button, making sure that Brad couldn't hear our conversation.

"You can't do that," I hissed. I was sure that Brad couldn't hear me, but what if the phone wasn't working properly? "You shouldn't impersonate a police officer."

Nanna smiled beatifically. "I'm a

confused old woman, what are they gonna do? Besides, no-one'll ever find out."

I was about to tell her that it was illegal, and she could get into serious trouble, but before I could say anything, Nanna hit the speaker button again.

"Sorry about that," she said. "We really appreciate your cooperation in all this. I know it must be very difficult for you. Were you and your sister very close?"

There was a split second of silence, and for a moment, I wondered if Brad had caught on to us. But then he spoke with a sob in his voice, "Yes, it was just the two of us growing up. Dad died when we were young and our mother brought us up. And then, Mom died three years ago, and we moved to Vegas together. Charlene and I were always best friends."

Nanna murmured sympathetically. "I'm so sorry for your loss. This won't take more than a moment. Just to verify, is there anyone you can think of who might have wanted to hurt Charlene?"

"No," said Brad instantly. "Charlene didn't have many close friends after she moved here, and she wasn't dating anyone. She got on well with everyone at work, and I think she liked her roommates."

"And had she been acting strangely in the days before she died?"

"No, not at all."

"And I know this must be difficult for you, but where were you on the night she was killed?"

"I was having dinner with my partner Chris. He came over to my place at around six, and he left after eleven o'clock."

"Can you think of anyone, or anything about Charlene that had been unusual in the last few days?"

"No, like I said before, nothing at all. The only thing was this guy Andrew—she'd never told me about him before. But then, she never talks about her love life much. I don't think she's had a relationship that worked out beyond the first date or two since we moved to Vegas."

Nanna glanced me and Ian, but we both shook our heads. I couldn't think of anything else to ask—it seemed like there was nothing we could learn from Brad.

"Thanks for your help," Nanna said, "and before I hang up, there are two private investigators who are looking into Charlene's death as well. Andrew hired them. Would you be interested in chatting with them for a few minutes?"

"No!" Brad's voice was harsh. "I don't want to talk to anyone else. This has been difficult enough for me—I don't need people prying into my private life. Was that all for today?"

His tone had changed dramatically, and Nanna quickly said, "Yes, thank you so much."

She hung up, and then I turned to her and said, "You shouldn't have done that!"

Nanna shrugged. "You can honestly say you had nothing to do with the call. It was all me. And no-one's going to know I even made the call. Besides, you can see that Brad wouldn't have talked to you if it hadn't been for my help."

"She does have a point there," Ian pointed out.

I sighed. "You're right. At least now we know that Brad couldn't have been involved in any way—or his partner Chris."

"What's next?" Nanna asked. "Are you going to go talk to Charlene's roommates?"

"No, I've got the night off, so I think I'm going to go talk to Charlene's co-workers at the Treasury. I can talk to her roommates during the day between my shifts."

"That sounds great!" Nanna beamed at me. "I can come with you too."

I shook my head quickly. "I'm afraid not. Most of the girls who work as cocktail waitresses are acquaintances of mine, but I've never talked to them too much. I don't want them to get distracted by your presence."

Nanna nodded thoughtfully. "You're right. I can be quite the distraction. I hope you find out something useful tonight."

CHAPTER 8

*I*t was a bit strange going to the Treasury on my night off, but Ian and I walked through the brightly lit casino pit and smiled at some of the dealers and waitresses we knew.

The pit was as lively as ever, bursting with the energy and excitement of the gamblers. There were occasional whoops of glee, and loud, sharp bursts of laughter. Chimes from the slot machines ran out, and every now and then, a shriek of happy surprise pierced the air.

Ian and I made our way past the enthusiastic tourists, winding our way through the rows of slot machines until we found the door marked "staff only" and pushed our way through. Ian wasn't technically staff, but he was here with someone who was, and I knew it would be fine.

The employee break room at the Treasury Casino was a fraction of the size of the casino pit, but it was still as large as a couple of one-bedroom apartments put together. There was a kitchenette area with three refrigerators, four microwaves, a toaster, two coffee pots, and cabinets for storing things. Near the kitchen area were a few round, white dining tables with plastic chairs arranged around them. On the other side of the room, there was a large flat screen TV, put on mute and showing some talking head with subtitles scrolling below. Leather lounges were arranged near the TV, and I spotted my friend Alba sitting by herself on one of the love seats.

I made a beeline for her, and waved happily when she saw me.

Alba was my closest friend out of all the waitresses who worked in the Treasury. We'd been working together a long time, our shifts often coincided, and we both seemed to share the same sense of humor.

Alba was tall, with a plus-sized hourglass figure and flaming red hair. Her hair clashed with the red and white uniform that the cocktail waitresses wore, but she still looked stunning, and I knew that her beauty extended deep within her heart.

"Tiffany!" she said cheerfully as I drew closer. "I thought today was your night off."

"It is." I settled down on an armchair near her. Ian sat on the chair next to me, and I introduced him to Alba. "We're looking into the death of one of the waitresses, Charlene Nelson—did you know her?"

Alba raised one eyebrow at me. "You've been hired to look into her death?"

I nodded. "Just yesterday."

Alba smiled cynically and leaned back. "That explains it. I can't imagine anyone else really caring about her death."

Alba was one of the sweetest people I knew, and her comment left me a bit shocked. "Why's that?"

"We all pretty much hated her here. She was mean, she was cunning and she was rude. She kept trying to get to any man who looked rich enough to tip well—it was all she seemed to be after. There are rumors that she went out with a few of the rich whales, and that she asked them to buy her things. Of course, they might just be rumors, but she wasn't a nice person either."

"How so?"

"Well, she was pleasant enough on the surface, but every now and then she'd throw in a subtle insult that was meant to put you down. She was good at it too, making you feel bad about yourself. I tried to avoid her as much as I could, and I know most of the other girls did too."

"Did you know much about her personal life?"

Alba shook her head. "Any time someone's rude to me for no reason, I try to avoid them. Charlene told me—what was it now?—that I wore the uniform well enough for someone with so much extra weight." She laughed cheerfully. "My extra pounds don't bother me, so I didn't care about what she said, but it did bother me that she tried to hurt my feelings. I never talked to her much after that—and that would be a year ago."

I nodded sympathetically. "That sounds horrible. I had no idea that she was actually a mean person—the guy who hired us seemed to have fallen in love with her."

Alba rolled her eyes. "Did he by any chance meet her at the Treasury?"

"Yes."

"Then I'm not surprised. I suppose those rumors about Charlene dating rich men who came to play at the Treasury were true."

"But it was just one man," Ian piped up. "He could've been an exception."

Alba shrugged. "Maybe. And even if she did date rich gamblers, that doesn't mean she deserved to be killed."

I said, "Who do you think would know more about her?"

Alba frowned and thought for a few minutes, and then she said, "That would be Jodie. You know her?"

I nodded. Jodie had joined the Treasury about six months ago; she was slim and petite, with shoulder-length straight blond hair.

"She and Charlene seemed to be like frenemies," Alba went on. "I would see them talking sometimes, and they seemed to be friendly enough. But then one day, I overheard Jodie telling Charlene that it was too bad she didn't have a boyfriend. Of course, men didn't like to go out with women who reeked of desperation."

I raised my eyebrows. "That's a pretty mean thing to say. Do you know what Charlene said to that?"

Alba laughed. "I think Charlene just ignored Jodie's comment. I wouldn't be friends with someone who had said something like that to me, but maybe Charlene was so mean that she didn't have any other friends and had to tolerate those kinds of comments. And I'm sure Jodie wouldn't say things like that if Charlene wasn't nasty back to her."

I tilted my head thoughtfully. "Do you know anyone else who might have been friends with Charlene?"

Alba shook her head. "Not really, but

look." She jerked her head toward the sofas on the other end of the room. "There's Jodie now. I'm sure she'll be more help than I was."

I'd only spoken to Jodie a few times before, so when Ian and I walked up, she didn't seem all that interested in talking to us.

I introduced Ian, and Jodie made a noncommittal noise. She pulled out her phone, and was about to start typing out a text, when I said, "We don't want to waste your time when you're on a break, but we're looking into Charlene's death. I heard you two were good friends."

Jodie looked at me and smiled. "Yes, Charlene was such a sweet girl."

I rolled my eyes. "That's not what we hear."

Jodie's blue eyes were wide with innocence. "What do you mean?"

"We heard you and Charlene were frenemies," Ian supplied. "That you'd hang out, but that you were mean to each other."

Jodie looked at us thoughtfully for a few minutes, and then she shrugged. "Sure, I guess you could say that. Charlene didn't have many friends, and I tried to be nice to her, but she wasn't always nice to me."

"I heard you weren't nice to her either."

Jodie's eyebrows shot up. "Hang on, are you trying to say that I killed her? Because I didn't!"

"I wasn't saying that," I said quickly. "I know you wouldn't do anything like that."

"*I* don't know that," Ian said stubbornly. "Where were you when Charlene was killed?"

"I was at home by myself," Jodie said. "But I had no reason to kill her. She was my friend."

"I know," I said reassuringly. I sent Ian a warning glance. "We just want you to tell us what you know about Charlene. Did she have any other friends at the Treasury? Or any other friends that you know of?"

Jodie shrugged. "She wasn't good at making friends. At least, she wasn't good at keeping them. She would be sweet for a day or two, but then she'd say something mean, and people wouldn't want to hang out with her. Same with the boys. She couldn't keep a boyfriend for too long."

"So, you knew about her love life."

Jodie glanced at her phone longingly, and then turned back to me. "I knew she didn't have a boyfriend. Ever since I'd known her, she'd gone out on a date or two, but the guys never stuck around. Of course, that's because…"

Her voice trailed off, and she looked at me warily.

"It's okay," I said encouragingly. "You won't get into trouble if you tell me. I've already heard that Charlene dated gamblers who came to the casino."

Jodie played with a strand of her hair. "She wouldn't come out and admit it, but I think she was looking for a rich guy to snag. If she thought that a man was rich enough, she'd go out with him—but they were all out-of-towners. I'm not sure how she expected a relationship like that last."

"Did she have any ex-boyfriends that you knew of?"

Jodie knit her brows thoughtfully. "I've

only been here for six months, and she never mentioned any exes to me."

"And what about her roommates?"

"They seemed okay—I went over to her apartment once because she'd left her scarf behind, and I wanted to drop it off. I can tell you their names if you'd like."

"Yes please," I said, pulling my notebook out of my bag. "And her address."

Jodie told me all the details, and then she said, "I can't believe this happened to Charlene. I mean, she didn't really have any friends that I knew of, but I don't think she had any enemies either. She didn't get out all that much."

"So you don't know if maybe someone hated her, or was threatening her?"

Jodie shook her head, no.

"What about her behavior before she died?" I said. "Was she acting strangely in any way?"

"No," Jodie said. "Everything about her had seemed to be normal."

We asked Jodie a few more questions about Charlene's behavior, and who else might know a bit more about her. Jodie reeled off the names of a couple more cock-tail waitresses, and then after a while, Ian and I said goodbye to her, and headed off to chat with Charlene's other co-workers.

Some of the waitresses Jodie had mentioned were on break, but others were at work. Ian and I talked to a few of them; despite our efforts, we learned nothing new.

We left the breakroom and traipsed over to the bar where we saw Diane, one of the waitresses who Jodie had mentioned as having talked to Charlene once or twice. Diane seemed happy to help, and she took a five-minute break to chat with us at the bar, telling us everything she knew about Charlene—which wasn't much. Charlene didn't have any enemies that Diane knew of, or any boyfriends, and hadn't been acting strangely before her death.

I was disappointed by the lack of infor-mation, but we thanked Diane anyway, and then she trudged back to work.

Ian and I were about to walk back home, when I noticed a woman rushing toward me. She was tall, wearing purple leggings and a purple T-shirt, with blond hair streaked purple. It was the woman I'd noticed the other day!

She smiled, and said, "Hello! I'm Belinda, but my friends call me Billy."

"I'm Tiffany," I said, slightly mystified as to why she'd chosen to introduce herself.

As if reading my mind, Billy said, "I saw you asking around about that waitress who died. Charlene."

I peered at Billy curiously. "Did you know her?"

Billy shrugged. "I wouldn't really call it 'know.' But I've been hanging around the casino pit for a few days—I've decided to move to Vegas. It was meant to be just a vacation, but I've applied for a job here. Anyway, I've seen Charlene working here."

"And did you notice anything unusual about her when she was at work?"

Billy looked off into the distance for a few seconds, and then finally, she shook her head. "To be honest, not really. She always seemed very cheerful, you know, the kind of fake cheerful you have to be when you're a waitress. But I noticed she'd flirt with some of the older men—you know, the ones who wear spiffy clothes and big watches."

I nodded. "That seems par for the course for a waitress."

"I've heard the other waitresses telling you that Charlene used to flirt with rich-looking men and try to get dates with them. I think they're right."

"Maybe," I said noncommittally. "Did you notice anything else about Charlene when you were at the pit?"

Billy shook her head. "No, but that's not the reason I wanted to talk to you. See, I've decided I'm going to help you guys out in your investigation."

I smiled at her politely. Billy seemed like a reasonably intelligent person. She wore subtle makeup, and she looked clean and pretty, though a tad too purple-themed for my tastes. I didn't know why she was offering to help me, but I didn't need any more people tagging along; Ian and Nanna were more than enough for me.

"I appreciate the offer," I said trying not to sound annoyed. "But I've got Ian to help me, and I work better without too many people around."

"But I can be really good as an investigator," Billy said enthusiastically. "I know tae kwon do, and I'm a pretty good shot. I'm good at talking to people, and I don't have a job now, so I'd be happy to help you out until I get a job and move here permanently."

Her enthusiasm was starting to grate. Ian and I exchanged a glance—while Billy didn't have any obvious signs of craziness, her eagerness seemed a bit suspicious. I wondered if she was involved in Charlene's death in any way, and as if he'd read my mind, Ian said, "Did you ever talk to Charlene?"

"No," Billy said, "but I didn't know she was about to get killed."

"And where were you on Sunday, between seven and nine at night?"

Billy looked at me, hurt. "You think I killed her? That's ridiculous. I just came over to offer you my help. I didn't think you'd accuse me of killing her."

"But where were you?"

"I was right here, at the casino pit. Is that what you wanted, an alibi? You can probably check the surveillance tapes, don't you have surveillance tapes on all the casinos?" She brightened up suddenly. "I bet I'd be great working in casino security!"

"Maybe you would," I said trying to feign enthusiasm for her idea. Ian and I slipped past her, and started heading out, but Billy walked after us.

"Don't just leave! Aren't there more people you need to talk to? I can talk to people if you'd like me to."

I turned around and looked at her seriously. "Please don't talk to people about Charlene's death. If you do, the cops might think it's suspicious, and I don't want you getting into trouble."

"I won't get into any trouble," Billy said. "I just want to help you guys out."

I could see I wouldn't be able to shake off easily, so I smiled and nodded. "Why don't you give me a night to think about it? I'll get back to you on that."

Ian and I walked off rapidly, and I could

hear her saying, "But I haven't even given you my phone number."

Just then, one of the bouncers glanced my way, and saw Billy trailing after me. He paced off rapidly, and I knew he would use some polite pretext to keep Billy from following me out.

When Ian and I had gotten almost halfway home, Ian finally said, "Well, that was odd."

"That's kind of how you started working with me," I reminded him. "I ran into your apartment to hide from that maniac trying to kill me, and then you sort of insisted on helping me out."

"But she seems different," Ian said. "There seems to be something wrong about her."

I grinned. "Are you saying there's nothing wrong with you?"

Ian smiled back. "No, that's not what I mean. I think... isn't her timing strange?"

A sudden shiver ran down my spine. "You don't think she's working for Eli, do you?"

Ian shook his head quickly. "No, I don't

think that. I just meant—she seems to think that investigating is glamorous and fun. It's not."

"No," I agreed. "But maybe we don't need to worry about her. I think she was just looking for a fun thing to do on vacation. She'll probably have a nice buffet dinner, go to a show, and play some slots— and then she'll forget all about this idea. I'll probably never even see her again."

"I hope we don't see her," Ian agreed. "I've got a bad feeling about her."

CHAPTER 9

The next morning, I texted Ian to come over so we could have breakfast together in my apartment. A few minutes after I sent the text, Ian showed up carrying Snowflake under one arm, and a large box under the other. He placed Snowflake on the floor, and the box on top of the countertop.

Snowflake came over to me and meowed, so I took the hint and bent down to pet her. Ian opened the lid of the box, and I peered into it and gasped with delight.

"Those look amazing!"

Ian beamed. "Glenn came by earlier this morning, and said he made a few too many when Wes and Nanna came to visit him yesterday."

"I'm so glad he did! I've never eaten homemade Danishes before."

"Neither have I! I asked Glenn how long it took him to make them, and he just laughed. He said he used to make them when he was younger and had first started working at a bakery—they smell so amazing!"

I stopped petting Snowflake, and went over to the countertop to admire Glenn's creations more closely. They were square, with fluffy, glazed edges, and a center of fruit filling. There were three different fillings—apricot, blueberry, and apple.

Snowflake meowed plaintively, and I glanced back at her. "Sorry, Snowflake. I can't keep these Danishes waiting any longer—but I promise we'll play as soon as I've finished eating."

I washed my hands and set out the pastries on plates for Ian and me, while he made us each a mug of steaming hot coffee.

Ian and I settled down on the couch, and for a long time, the only sound in the room was that of us sipping our coffees and chomping away on the Danishes. Snowflake sat next to us, and looked from Ian to me, giving us both dirty looks. She wasn't interested in the pastries, but she did want us to hurry up and play with her.

Finally, Ian and I came up for air.

"These are the best Danishes I've ever had!"

I agreed. "The fruit filling is just perfect, and there's some custard in the corners as well—I'm not sure how to explain it, but everything just goes together so perfectly."

There were only two Danishes left—one for me, and one for Ian. We both slowed down our chewing, and savored our last pastry slowly.

When we finally finished our delicious breakfast, I made us some more coffee, and then Ian and I sat and talked about the case. As I sipped my coffee, Snowflake jumped onto my lap, and I stroked her soft, fluffy coat.

"I'm glad Nanna called Brad and spoke to him on the phone," Ian said. "He seems really opposed to talking to anyone about his sister's death. If he hadn't been Charlene's brother, I would've thought he was trying to hide something. But he seems to have a rock-solid alibi as well—I'm sure the police have checked it out."

I nodded. "But it wouldn't hurt to double check."

"Do you think we should try to talk to Brad later?"

I shrugged. "It's always important to talk to family members if you can. Family members are suspects by default, and Brad might be able to tell us something we didn't know before. Maybe we could talk to the rest of the people we need to, and then we'll try to find him at his laundromat."

"Speaking of the laundromat, maybe we should try to speak with Brad's partner, Chris. Even if Brad doesn't want to talk to us, maybe Chris will."

"You're right. I guess the easiest place to start is with the roommates. We can head over there as soon as we've finished our coffee."

~

*C*harlene's apartment was a short drive from my place—she lived slightly northeast of where I did, and I guesstimated that it would take her half an hour to walk to the Treasury. The rent on her apartment was probably a bit cheaper than mine, but she would have still been able to walk to and from work.

I parked my car on the street, and then Ian and I got out and looked at the building where Charlene lived. It was run down and somewhat decrepit, with paint that was peeling and fading under the harsh Nevada sun. Many of the buildings on this street looked similar—old and tired apartments with small parking lots in front, and stairs that ran up the outside of the building. I was about to walk over to Charlene's building, when I spotted a familiar face.

Billy smiled at me and Ian, and waved brightly. "Tiffany! Ian! How nice to run into you."

I'd been so busy staring at Charlene's apartment that I hadn't noticed where Billy had shown up from.

I gaped at her. "What are you doing here?"

"I was just out for a drive. I'm glad I saw you two here."

I raised an eyebrow at her. "So this was just a coincidence?"

Billy beamed at me brightly. "I'd say it was more of a fated kind of thing—I think I must've moved to Vegas to be able to help you guys out. I heard that the guy who hired you called Charlene his lucky charm. Maybe I'll be your lucky charm?"

I eyed her warily. She didn't seem to be armed, and she didn't look particularly dangerous, but her presence made me feel a bit uneasy. I wasn't about to trust her, and I certainly wasn't about to spend any more time with her.

"It was nice to run into you," I said, mustering up as much cheerfulness as I could. "But I just remembered I have to go somewhere else."

Billy's face fell. "Where? Maybe I could come with you."

"I don't think so," I said. "Come on, Ian."

"Wait," Billy said plaintively. "Don't go! I

could help you guys with your work. And I know lots of martial arts—I could protect you and act like a bodyguard if you need one."

I didn't feel like telling Billy that my friend Stone had forced me to take Krav Maga lessons and to learn how to shoot a gun. Instead, I said, "I'm all set for body-guards for now, thanks."

And then, before Billy could try to persuade me to let her help out on our case, Ian and I jumped into the car and drove off. I meandered around the side streets for a bit, and then I drove back to Charlene's apartment. Once again, I parked on the street. This time, Ian and I sat in the car for a full minute, waiting to see if anyone followed us, but there seemed to be no one on our tail.

Finally, Ian said, "I can't believe Billy just came out of nowhere."

I shook my head, berating myself. "I should've been more careful—it was such a short drive, I didn't even think to check if someone was following me."

"You don't think she's working for Eli,

do you?" And then, as though talking to himself, Ian said, "No, that can't be. Eli would have hired someone much more capable and confident—Billy seems silly and unprofessional. Unless it's all just an act."

I chewed my inner lip thoughtfully. "I don't think she's working for Eli. She's just a bit strange. You do meet a lot of strange people in Vegas."

Ian and I got out of the car and again headed over to Charlene's apartment. It was on the second floor, and I hadn't called ahead to announce my arrival. We knocked loudly, and a few minutes later, a twenty-something-year-old woman answered the door.

Her dark blond hair was messy, and she wore pajamas and looked at us blearily. "What?"

"I'm sorry to have woken you," I said quickly. "You must be one of Charlene's roommates."

The woman looked from me to Ian. "You're not with the police, are you?"

I shook my head. "We're private investigators, and we've been hired by someone who met Charlene while she was alive. I'm really sorry to have woken you."

The woman stretched, and yawned loudly. "No, it's fine. Come in, I wanted to get up early anyway, so I could run some errands before my shift started this evening. It can get inconvenient when you work odd hours."

"Tell me about it," I said, as I followed the woman inside. "I work as a dealer at the Treasury, and I'm always having a hard time getting everything I want to do, done."

The inside of the apartment was shabby, but clean. The carpet was an indeterminate dark shade, and the sofas looked well-used, as though they'd been purchased second-hand. An abstract, floral-looking print hung on one wall, and a flat-screen TV was nestled against the other. Ian and I sat down on the sofa, and then the woman said, "I'm Christine by the way. I'll go change, and then we can chat."

She got up and disappeared through a room that I assumed led to her bedroom, and was gone for a few minutes, before reappearing again, this time, dressed in shorts and a tank top. She tied her hair back into a low ponytail, and she headed over to the kitchen adjoining the living room. As she busied herself with making coffee, she said, "What did you guys want to know?"

"Just anything at all that you can tell us about Charlene," I said.

"Who hired you guys?"

"A man named Andrew Combs. He met Charlene at the Treasury."

Christine finished making her coffee, and headed back to the living room. "He met her once, and he decided to hire you guys?"

"No," I said, before Ian could jump in and explain how Andrew had fallen in love. "They went on a few dates together."

Christine shrugged. "Yeah, sounds about right."

"What do you mean?"

"There'd been a couple of men who Charlene had met through work. She told me that work wasn't a bad place to meet guys, but I knew that she was trying to get herself a rich husband. She wouldn't come out and admit it, but she only dated people with money."

"So she'd gone out with quite a few men recently?"

Christine shook her head. "She hadn't told me about Andrew. But before that, earlier in the month, she went out for drinks with some guy, but that didn't work out. Her last date would have been a month or so before that."

"Did she tell you much about these men?"

Christine took a sip of her coffee and stared into her mug thoughtfully. "Once in a while, she'd be really hopeful about a man, and tell me that he seemed charming and successful. I'd tell her to get real, and try to go out with someone who lived in Vegas—not some tourist who would fly out the very next day. But she never listened."

"Maybe one of those men she dated came back to Vegas, and tried to see her again."

Christine shook her head. "No, if that had happened, Charlene wouldn't hesitate to gloat. She thought I was being too cynical, and too quick to tell her to settle. One time she did go out with someone local, but that didn't work out."

"When was this?"

"About two years ago—Charlene dated a valet at the Treasury, Vince."

"Vince... That name sounds familiar. Maybe he still works at the Treasury."

"I wouldn't know," Christine said. "They were together for six months or so, but I don't think Charlene was faithful to him. Once it was over, Charlene didn't seem too upset—it was like she knew the relationship was doomed from the start."

I nodded, and made a note to look up Vince. "Do you know anything about this Vince? His full name, or where he lives?"

"I think his full name was Vince Valmary. But I don't know anything more than that."

"And what about your other roommate? Is she home now?"

Christine shook her head. "No, she works most days at the Swinton Ladies Boutique near the mall in South Vegas. She should be home soon after lunch today, if you want to come by then to talk to her."

I nodded. "I'll do that. But back to Charlene—what was she like?"

Christine savored the last sip of her coffee, and then looked down at her empty mug in disappointment. "I'm going to make myself another mug," she announced, before getting up and heading back to the kitchen.

As she made another cup, she said, "Charlene wasn't my favorite person, but she was a good roommate. She did her share of the cleaning, and she never let the dirty dishes pile up. I knew she didn't have too many friends, and she wasn't a particularly friendly person, but she paid her share of the rent on time, and I guess that's what really counts when it comes to roommates."

"But you two seem to have gotten along."

"We've been living together for two and a half years. The other roommates come and go, but Charlene and I both work shifts at different casinos—she worked at the

Treasury, and I work at the Mirage. So I guess, in a way, we understood each other."

"These other roommates who came and went, how many of them knew Charlene?"

Christine tilted her head and looked off to one side thoughtfully. "There was Zara... and then Michelle. Candy—no, she was before Charlene moved in." Christine thought some more, and finally counted them off on her fingers. "Zara, Michelle, Darlene and Angelina."

"Do you have phone numbers and details for them?"

Christine nodded, and whipped out her phone. She recited full names and phone numbers, and I jotted down everything and repeated it all back to her to verify.

"I don't think they'd have kept in touch with Charlene, though," Christine said. "Vegas isn't that kinda place. People move on. They leave you behind."

I sighed and agreed with her, and Ian said, "That's why it's so hard to make friends here. Everyone keeps moving around and not staying in touch."

"Yeah," said Christine. "And it's hard to

make new friends if you're busy working all the time."

I thought through what I'd learned about Charlene so far. "Did you know of anyone who really hated Charlene? Enough to want to hurt her?"

"No, she didn't have many friends, but that doesn't mean she had enemies. I can't think of anyone who would hate her enough to want to hurt her."

"And what about the days before she died? Was she acting strangely in any way?"

"No, not that I can think of."

"What about this planned trip to New York of hers?" I asked, remembering what Andrew had said. "Did you know that she was planning to go?"

Christine smiled and shook her head. "No, I don't think she was planning to go at all. That was a line she used on men she'd just met—she told them that she would be visiting their hometown soon. I think she said it to see whether they were looking for a serious relationship or not, or if they'd get scared that she would show up on their doorstep. It was just one of those tricks she used—it's hard to meet men, and even harder if you're constantly meeting people who don't live where you do."

The three of us chatted a bit more about Charlene, and life in Vegas, but we didn't learn anything useful. Finally, we said goodbye, and that we'd drop by after lunch to talk to her other roommate, Mary.

Before we left, I handed Christine my card. "Call me if you think of anything else."

"I will," Christine said, taking my card. "But I don't think there's anything else to say—Charlene was just such an ordinary person. In many ways, she was just like me —she lived here, she tried to make a living, and she tried to find a nice man who she could settle down with. I can't imagine why anyone would bother to kill her."

Ian and I headed back to my car. This time, I took a good look around before I got in and drove off. There seemed to be no sign of Billy, and I hoped that perhaps she'd given up and decided to leave me and Ian alone.

CHAPTER 10

$\mathcal{J}$an and I drove over to Charleston Heights, where Brad's laundromat was. As I drove, I kept an eye out for anyone who might be following me, but I didn't see anything suspicious.

Sunset Laundry was in a large strip mall, next to a seedy looking bar that promised cheap drinks and video poker. The other establishments included a McDonalds, a Mexican food place, a hair salon, and a tax accountant.

The laundromat was tinier inside than it looked from the outside. There was a bench where customers could sit and wait, and at least five washers and dryers. A machine dispensed washing powder, and there was a countertop designed for folding clothes.

Everything was coin-operated, and there was a tiny desk near the back of the room, next to a door that I assumed led to the back office.

Two men were at the desk, talking to each other in hushed tones. I wondered if they might be Brad and Chris—one of the men was sitting behind the desk and he wouldn't do that if he wasn't an employee or an owner of the place.

The sole patron of the place, a large muscular man with a gray, chest-length beard and multiple tattoos was loading his clothes into a machine. We waited 'til he was done and had walked out of the laundromat, and then Ian and I headed over to the two men who were watching us with mild disinterest.

"You can get change at the bar next door," one of the men said. He was short, and slightly chubby, with close-cropped blond hair. The man next to him had the tall, lithe body of a dancer, and straight, jet black hair.

"We don't need change," I said. "We're trying to talk to the owners, Brad and Chris."

The short man I'd been talking to eyed us warily, and the tall man said, "You found them. I'm Chris, and this is Brad."

I looked carefully at Chris. There was a hard, suspicious edge to his voice, and I wondered if he thought Ian and I were trying to sell something.

"Ian and I are private investigators," I said. "We've been hired to look into Charlene's death."

Chris's eyes grew cold, and he pressed his lips together.

"We're not talking to you," Brad said quickly. His face had turned red, and he glared at us and crossed his arms over his chest.

"I'm very sorry for your loss," I said to Brad. "It must be terrible, losing a sister you were so close with growing up."

"Get out."

This time, it was Chris who had spoken. His words were icy, and while Brad looked like he might explode at any moment, Chris seemed calm but full of hatred.

"We'd just like a few minutes," I tried again. "We know how much Brad loved his sister, and we've been hired to pull out all the stops to find out who did this."

"We're not talking to you," Brad repeated. "If you're not here to wash your clothes, you need to get out."

Ian and I exchanged a glance.

I looked at Chris, who jerked his head toward the door, and then at Brad. The anger in Brad's eyes had faded slightly, and was replaced with a tinge of sadness. He met my gaze, and shook his head. "I'm not talking about it."

"Just a minute or two," I pleaded. "It might help our investigation."

"You heard him," Chris growled. "Get out now, before I have to call the cops on you."

Ian and I didn't need any more encouragement. We finally turned, and got back into the car.

"That was disappointing," Ian said, as I started the engine.

"Tell me about it."

"If Nanna hadn't called Brad, this would probably be all we'd ever have gotten out of them."

"I'm not about to give up so easily," I said. "I don't know how we'll get them to talk to us, but we'll figure something out."

When we got back to my apartment, Ian ordered Chinese takeout for lunch, and as we ate, I fired up my laptop and logged into my private investigator's database.

"I don't like this Billy girl," I explained to Ian. "I know her name's Belinda, but I don't have a second name. I'd like to look her up, see what kind of background she's got."

"You could ask someone at the Treasury," Ian suggested. "Billy said she'd been hanging out there for the last few days."

"That's a good idea," I said, and I gave my friend Alba a quick call, explaining what I wanted.

Alba wasn't at work, but she said she'd seen Billy around, and had seen her chatting with her friend Melissa. She promised to find out what she could, and then give me a call back.

Alba called me back just as Ian and I had finished our lunch. "I found out a few things," Alba said. "Her real name's Belinda Marks, and she's originally from Connecticut. I've also got her phone number, and I can tell you why she broke up with her last boyfriend."

I laughed. "I guess she's been chatting with the girls about her love life?"

"That's right, you know how some people get after they've had a few drinks. Apparently, there was one day when Billy got drunk and poured out her life story to Jessica. Hold on, I'll get you her phone number first."

I grabbed a pen and paper, and copied down the string of numbers that Belinda recited, and then repeated them back to her. "Yep, that's it," Alba said. "And actually, her love life isn't all that interesting in some ways. Her last boyfriend cheated on her with her best friend, and the boyfriend before that dumped her for a nineteen-year-old who had just graduated high school. She says she's over men and moved to Vegas to start a new life. She's not sure what she wants to do, but she wants to be helpful and make people's lives better."

"She sounds like someone who's had a bit of a rough patch," I said. "I really appreciate you digging up all this information for me."

"No problem," Alba said. "Are you coming in to work tonight?"

"Yes, my shift starts at seven."

We chatted for a few minutes, and then after I hung up, I told Ian what I'd learned.

Ian popped into his apartment to grab his laptop, and then we both began tapping away on our keyboards. Ian was looking up Belinda on social media, and I was looking her up in my private investigator's database.

An hour later, we both logged off, and I made us some coffee while we filled each other in on what we'd learned so far.

I went first. "Belinda's got some priors. She's been arrested for assault, but she got off with community service. She graduated high school a few years back, and since then, she's worked a series of jobs—waitress, kitchen hand, Uber driver. She grew up in the foster care system, and she moved around a lot. From what I've learned of her, she doesn't seem like someone I can trust—she doesn't sound all that dangerous, but I don't think I should be flattered that she's chosen to follow me around."

"Belinda's love life checks out, too," Ian said. "It's just what Alba told you—she seems to have had two serious boyfriends in her life, and neither of them worked out. I'm not sure that getting arrested for assault is such a big deal these days."

"It means she's got a temper on her, and she's impulsive."

"And that she was dumb enough to get arrested, and to not be able to wipe it off her record. Maybe that means she's not someone who's working for Eli?"

I looked at Ian thoughtfully. "You have a point there—I wouldn't expect Eli to hire anyone with an obvious criminal record."

"And if she really is someone who's had a bit of bad luck, she might lose interest in you pretty quickly."

"That's what I'm hoping for."

~

*A*fter a quick chat about what we'd learned of Charlene so far, Ian and I decided to set out for Charlene's apartment to talk to her other roommate, Mary. We stepped out of the apartment and were walking across the parking lot to where I'd left my car, when a flash of blonde and purple darted out from between the cars.

"Tiffany! Please let me help you."

"Billy!" I mentally kicked myself for somehow having missed where she'd been hiding between the cars. "I don't need your help. I mean, I appreciate you asking and everything."

"But I'm really good at talking to people, and being persistent," Billy said. "See, I managed to get you to talk to me a couple of times today."

"I know you think you're being helpful," I said calmly. "But I really can't have you tagging along with me, or showing up like this. I investigate a lot of dangerous people, and you could get yourself hurt."

Billy shook her head. "No, I wouldn't get hurt. I'd keep *you* from getting hurt."

Ian and I exchanged a glance.

"You really don't want to come along with us," Ian said. "Most of our work is very boring."

"I don't mind that," Billy said, grinning enthusiastically. "I'm used to boring work. And I know I can help you guys out if you just let me."

I glanced at my watch. My patience was running thin, and if Billy was somehow working for Eli, I didn't want to risk getting in trouble. If she wasn't working for Eli, and was just someone looking for a change of pace, I didn't want to have to be responsible for her.

I tried to rein in my annoyance. "I've said no about a hundred times now, Billy. I'm not going to repeat myself—I don't want you following us around, and if I see you again, I'm going to have to get a restraining order."

Billy's face fell. She looked like a little puppy who'd just been kicked, and she brushed back her hair with one hand and tilted up her chin. "I'm not going to take no for an answer. I know you think you don't need my help—and you probably haven't needed my help before—but I'm going to hang around, and see what I can do to make your life better."

"You can make my life better by leaving us alone," I grumbled under my breath as Ian and I got into my car. For some reason, I hadn't wanted to say that out loud—maybe it was the hangdog look Billy had just given me.

As I pulled out of the parking lot, I looked into my rearview mirror, and noticed Billy standing there, watching us drive off.

When we knocked on Charlene's apartment, the door was opened by a young woman who had chin length, jet black hair cut into a short bob. She had multiple piercings, dark eyeliner, and wore a black tank top with black shorts. She also wore an annoyed expression, which I assumed was part of the goth look.

"You must be Tiffany and Ian," she said

sulkily. "Christine told me you'd be stopping by. Come in."

Although she'd just invited us in, Mary seemed anything but pleased to see us. The three of us sat in the living, and Mary crossed one leg over the other and eyed us distastefully.

"I'm not sure how I can help," she said. "I didn't really know her well."

"How long did you know her for?"

"I moved in six months ago. They had some other roommates before me, maybe you'd want to talk to them."

I nodded. "Maybe we will. But in the meantime, we really appreciate you talking to us. I know you think there's nothing to tell, but anything could help us out. Why don't you start by telling us what you thought of Charlene?"

Mary shrugged. "She seemed nice."

"Were you friends?"

"No."

"But you must've chatted with her sometimes."

"Not really."

I stifled an exasperated sigh that was

trying to make its way out. "What did she seem like, other than being nice?"

"I never saw her much. I work during the day at a clothing store, and Charlene worked nights mostly."

"Okay, but did you know anything about Charlene's friends, or her love life?"

"No."

"What about her family? Did you ever meet Charlene's brother Brad, or his partner, Chris?"

Something flickered in Mary's eyes, but she shook her head. "No."

"You've never met them, not even once?"

"No."

We were getting nowhere. "What about her behavior before she died? Did Charlene act unusual in any way?"

"No."

I took a deep breath, determined to forge ahead with my usual questions. "And what about any enemies? Did you know of anyone who might've wanted to hurt Charlene?"

"No."

That exasperated sigh finally left my body in a sharp, short whoosh. So far, the only answer we'd gotten out of Mary was, "No."

Ian said, "Is there any reason you don't want to talk to us?"

Mary turned her eyes sharply from me to him. She shrugged. "I don't know anything."

"Then you can tell us what you know."

"Which is nothing."

Ian and I stayed there for a few more minutes, trying in vain to get Mary to tell us anything—anything at all about Charlene. But she wouldn't budge, giving us monosyllabic answers, and insisting that she didn't know anything about Charlene.

Ian and I left feeling like we'd spent half an hour banging our heads against a large rock.

Ian said, "I wonder what her problem is."

"Maybe she doesn't like private investigators."

"Seems to me she's the kind of person who doesn't like people in general."

I glanced both ways down the street, before getting into my car again. I couldn't see Billy anywhere and there was no way she'd know where we'd gone, but it didn't hurt to be safe.

"It's not just that Mary dislikes people," I said, before we drove off. "I'm sure she's hiding something. When I asked her about Brad and Chris, she looked for a second like she was about to say something."

"I noticed that too!"

"If she's hiding something, we need to find out what it is."

"I'll find out for you. I know you have to catch up on your sleep during the day, but tomorrow, during the day, I'm going to run surveillance on Mary. Maybe that way I can uncover whatever she's hiding."

~

That night at the casino as I dealt out cards and made witty banter with the players, my mind drifted off to the case. Who would've wanted

Charlene dead? By all accounts, she was a rather unremarkable girl.

I watched the cocktail waitresses as they scurried about with their drink orders, and laughed and chatted with the gamblers. The jingles of the slot machines filled the air, and happy tourists laughed and went from one table to another.

Being friendly was part of the job description for a waitress, just as it was for the dealers. People often met potential spouses at work, and it wasn't all that unusual for a girl to want to marry someone who was successful and could take care of her. In fact, my very first client had been a former stripper who'd married a casino owner—I didn't think that marrying someone was a substitute for a career, but I tried not to judge those who considered it an alternative to working hard themselves. From what I'd heard, Charlene's attempts at marrying into money hadn't gone well—at least, not until she'd met Andrew.

As I watched, a large, florid man wearing a Hawaiian print shirt waved a waitress over and began to talk animatedly, waving his arms about. He looked slightly angry, and the waitress smiled, said something, and then scurried off. I wondered if the cops were right, that Charlene had been killed by someone who didn't know her all that well.

But then I thought back to the fact that neither Chris, Brad, nor Mary had wanted to talk to me. There must've been a reason behind their reticence. I suspected that Mary was hiding something, but maybe Brad was too upset to want to think about his sister's death. That didn't seem right to me though—if he really was mourning his sister's death, he would've wanted to find out the truth. I'd have to do take another stab at trying to talk to him and Chris.

When my shift was over, I found Ian waiting for me in in the lobby.

"You really don't have to keep walking me home," I said. "I'm sure I can take care of myself."

But we'd only taken a few paces forward when Billy rushed out of the crowd and over to us.

"Tiffany! Ian! I know you said not to

bother you, but I really do want to help you."

I was tired after my shift, and didn't feel as though my persuasion skills were quite up to par.

"It would be great if you could leave me alone," I said. "I don't want to be rude or upset you, but if you keep following me around like this, I'll start to think that *you* want to hurt me."

Belinda's jaw dropped, and she looked at me in shock. "I would never want to hurt you! I think it's great, how you're trying to find out who killed the cocktail waitress. I know you're working really hard, and most people wouldn't try so much."

"Look at it from my perspective," I told Belinda, as I continued to walk toward my apartment. "You keep popping up every-where, and you don't leave me alone."

"And I want to help you. If there's someone out there who wants to hurt you, they could get to you just as easily."

Belinda's words had an eerie ring of truth to them.

"I don't want you following me home," I

said. "If you really do want to help me, turn around and walk away—and I promise I'll have a good think about what you're saying."

Billy opened her mouth as though she was about to say something, but then she closed it again. She glanced from Ian to me, and then she finally said, "Okay. I don't want you to think that I'm a bad person, but I do want you to take my offer seriously. I feel like this is what I'm meant to do —that I'm meant to help you guys out. Just promise me you'll think about it."

"I promise," I said wearily. "Now, will you let us get home in peace and have some sleep?"

Billy nodded, and then she turned around and walked off.

"I'm surprised she left so easily," Ian said.

I shrugged. "It's just for now. I will think about letting her help us out, even though I don't want another person tagging along—I don't want to be responsible for someone else. I wonder what she'll do when I tell her no again."

CHAPTER 11

The next morning, I texted Ian once I was almost ready for breakfast. He came over to my apartment a few minutes later, but for once, he didn't have Snowflake with him.

"I left Snowflake with Tariq," Ian said, in response to my questioning gaze. "I feel really sorry for the man, and I think being with Snowflake cheers him up a bit. He must've gone through a lot."

"That's very considerate of you. How's he been settling in?"

Ian looked a bit guilty. "He's really nice, and he's always doing stuff. Like, last night, he asked me to go out and buy some groceries, and then he made us dinner—he made enough for about twenty people. He told me to freeze the leftovers, and that I could eat the food even when he wasn't around. That it might help me remember him."

I shuddered. "Why would you need to remember him? It sounds like he doesn't think he'll be around for very long."

Ian smiled, but his voice lacked its usual enthusiasm. "If you think about it, he and Stone probably need to leave soon to talk to the CIA officials and clear up Stone's record. And if that goes well, Tariq might not come back to Vegas."

"I guess that's the best possible scenario."

Ian started making coffee, and I looked in my fridge. I had three eggs in the carton, and a tiny bit of cheese. "I could make us cheese omelets," I said, "but I feel like having something sweet and comforting instead. The case we're investigating isn't going well so far, and I'm really worried about Stone. I know we can trust Tariq, but what if Eli and his men find out somehow that Tariq is here?"

Ian ignored my panic about Eli. "If you want something sweet, maybe I could go over to Neil's Diner, and pick up something to bring home? What do you feel like?"

I thought about it. Pancakes would be nice, or even a big, large cookie—although you probably weren't supposed to have cookies for breakfast. One or two couldn't hurt, right? Or maybe even a muffin...

I was weighing my options when there was a loud knock on the door. I opened it to find Nanna and Wes standing in the hallway.

Nanna was carrying a large Tupperware box, and she beamed at me. "Good morning! I figured you hadn't eaten breakfast, so I come bearing food."

She carried the box over to the countertop and opened it to reveal an assortment of muffins.

"Muffins! Perfect!"

"A muffin breakfast is always a good breakfast," Nanna said. "We stopped by Glenn's on our way up here, and he said to bring these for you."

There were at least a dozen muffins in

there, and Ian and I shared a knowing look. It would be a good idea to try to save two of the muffins to take the Tariq.

We all grabbed plates and mugs of coffee, and helped ourselves to the muffins. Nanna pointed out the different flavors, and I picked a white chocolate and raspberry muffin, and a chocolate chip muffin. We headed over to the couch to eat and chat, and I took a sip of coffee before biting into the first muffin.

The white chocolate and raspberry muffin was delicious. It was soft, fluffy, and the white chocolate was a wonderful, deep burst of sweetness, that paired perfectly with the slightly tart raspberry.

"Glenn and Karma would have come along," Wes was saying, "but Glenn wanted to go down to the specialty baking store down in South Vegas and pick up some ingredients. He said he couldn't be too late in getting there, or everything would be sold out—they're having some kind of sale right now."

"Maybe I could ask him to get me a few items," Ian said thoughtfully. "I've been meaning to get back into baking, but I haven't had time, not with this new case that we're working on."

"How's it going?" Nanna said between bites of her orange—poppy seed muffin.

I shook my head. "Not too good. So far, pretty much everyone who could have been a suspect has an alibi. And Charlene didn't get out all that much, so she couldn't have made enemies. She dated a few tourists, so she doesn't even have a steady boyfriend, or someone who could have been jealous and passionate enough to commit murder. We're going to try to follow up on some of those tourists she dated who went back home, but I think that's a long shot."

"She does have an ex-boyfriend she broke up with over a year ago," Ian quipped up. "But unless they'd secretly gotten together again, I can't see him having anything to do with her death."

"What about her roommates?" Nanna said. "What did they seem like?"

"Christine was nice," Ian said. "But the other roommate—Mary... that's right! I almost forgot to tell you, what with all the excitement of getting these delicious muffins and all."

I looked at Ian and raised one eyebrow. "You were planning to follow her today. Are you still going to do that?"

Ian shook his head vehemently. "I forgot to tell you! After you went to your shift yesterday, I headed back to Mary's place, just to see if she went out or anything. And she did! She went to a pawn shop over in Winchester, and I saw her getting out of a car carrying a bunch of handbags. I think they were designer ones. And then, I walked past the pawn shop and looked in, and I saw her showing the man at the counter a bunch of jewelry."

"Maybe she's having money troubles."

Ian shook his head. "No, something just seemed off about the whole thing. For one, Mary dresses in all black, and she has that kind of goth or emo thing going on, what-ever you call it these days. I can't imagine her carrying those colorful bags that she took into the pawn shop, or wearing the sort of jewelry she was trying to unload."

"Okay," I admitted. "It sounds a bit off.

But maybe this all-black thing is new to her, maybe she used to wear colorful clothes and bags."

"But expensive designer bags? And the jewelry looked expensive, too."

"That is suspicious," I admitted. "How would she able to afford designer bags and jewelry?"

"Mary wouldn't talk to us when we went to interview her," Ian said to Nanna. "She kept giving us monosyllabic replies. And she kept saying no to everything—that she didn't know anything about Charlene, and that she didn't know anyone who could hurt her. But I don't think she's telling us the truth. I wouldn't normally care about her pawning all these bags, but going to the pawn shop right after we went to talk to her? Something doesn't add up."

Nanna nodded sagely. "You're absolutely right. I think it was a good thing you followed Mary last night, instead of waiting for today. She ran off to the pawn shop right after you talked to her, so maybe these are things she needed to get rid of—maybe your showing up scared her."

"She didn't look all that scared when we showed up," I said. "She had that kind of arrogant, dismissive look that young kids have these days."

"That might all be an act," Wes said. "I've known lots of people who act extra tough when they get nervous or worried."

"We should go and talk to her again, maybe later today," Ian said.

I was just about to agree, when Nanna said, "That's not going to help! If she was rude and dismissive the first time you talked to her, she's not going to cooperate the next time."

"Maybe we should go see the pawn shop," Ian suggested. "We could talk to the man there, and have a look at the things Mary pawned."

"I've got an even better idea," Nanna said. "We should break into her apartment."

Wes looked at Nanna, a slightly shocked expression on his face. "That would be illegal!"

"Only if we get caught," Nanna said. She didn't seem to realize that she wasn't being logical. "I know Tiffany has this incredible set of lock picks, and she can break into buildings quite easily."

"And Mary lives in a pretty old building," Ian said, getting caught up by Nanna's enthusiasm. "I'm sure it would be easy to break in. And her stairs go up on the outside, so one of us could easily stand guard in case Mary comes back."

"When is she likely to be out?" Nanna said.

"Hang on!" I held up my hands, interrupting their break-in plans. "Wes is right—this is illegal."

"You're no fun!" Nanna said. "Do you want to solve this case or not?"

"I know Tiffany and Ian need to solve the case," Wes said. "But it's not a good idea to break into someone's apartment just because you saw them at a pawn shop."

"You're right," Nanna said, agreeing with Wes suddenly. But then, she turned to me, and dropped me a heavy wink.

I sighed. Nanna wasn't about to give up on this idea of hers, and I knew that she would bring it up again.

"What are your plans for the rest of the day?" Wes said to me.

"I think I'm going to run a couple of errands, and then, I'm going to talk to Charlene's ex-boyfriend at the Treasury in the afternoon. I asked around last night, and I know that his shift starts after lunch. I'm trying to time it so that I can talk to him, and then head straight to my own shift."

"We're going to go to yoga class with Karma," Nanna said. "And after that, we're having lunch with her and Glenn. Why don't Ian and you come along?"

"I would like that," I said. Glenn's cooking was hard to turn down. I turned to Ian. "What about you?"

Ian chewed his lip, and I knew he was wondering whether or not he should abandon Tariq. "I think that's a good idea," he said finally. "But maybe we should head over to Glenn's a bit early, and help him get things ready. I've got a friend who wouldn't mind having some leftovers for lunch—it's the least I could do for him," he added, looking at me. I knew that he meant he'd try to repay Tariq for all the cooking he'd done the night before.

"I'm sure Glenn would be happy to cook a bit extra for your friend," Wes said. "Then it's settled—we'll see you guys after we get back from the yoga class."

CHAPTER 12

*A*fter a delicious lunch at Glenn's, Ian and I headed back to our apartments. Glenn had packed some leftovers for Ian's "friend," but nobody pried too much about who this friend was. I spent some time cleaning out my apartment, and then I grabbed the bag I took with me to work, and speed-walked over to the Treasury.

Christine had described Charlene's ex, Vince Valmary, as extremely good-looking, and I recognized him as soon as we neared the valet station.

Vince was tall with broad shoulders and sandy brown hair. His eyes were green, specked with gold, and he had a mesmerizing smile. I watched as he handed over the keys to a sixty-something-year-old woman, pocketed a hefty tip, and then glanced over to us.

Ian and I took this as our cue, and walked over and introduced ourselves.

After the introductions were made, Vince looked at me and Ian curiously. "You don't really look like private investigators. Aren't they supposed to be angry middle-aged men who call all women 'dames?'"

I smiled and shook my head. "Only in film noir flicks. Ian and I have been doing this for a while now, and it's nothing like what you see in the movies."

Vince nodded. "I've got a few minutes to chat. I'll let my supervisor know I'm taking a five-minute break, and then I can help you out."

We waited near the entrance of the Treasury, until Vince came back, and gave us his undivided attention.

"What did you want to know?" he said, focusing his mesmerizing green eyes on me. "I hadn't talked to Charlene in a while, so there might not be too much I can say."

"But I heard you and Charlene had gotten together again," Ian bluffed. "Weren't you guys having a secret affair?"

Vince turned to Ian, a puzzled look on his face. "No, I'm dating Mindy, a waitress I met over in Summerlin. Mindy and I've been together for three months now, and I haven't talked to Charlene in over a year. Who's been feeding you those rumors?"

"Someone must've gotten confused," I said quickly. "So you're sure you haven't talked to Charlene recently?"

Vince shook his head, and I said, "Maybe Charlene wanted to get back with you?"

Vince let out a dry laugh. "No, she would never do that. Charlene knew what she wanted, and it wasn't a broke young man."

I raised one eyebrow. "And what did she want?"

"She was always after those moneybags visitors. But not too moneybags. She'd never go after those rich dudes who hang out at the high stakes poker tables. She told me once that someone who was too rich wouldn't make a good husband. She wanted someone who had maybe a couple of million in the bank, or a mid-six-figure salary—the kind of man who could support a family nicely, and probably still hang around on the weekends, instead of divorcing her for a newer model after five years."

"Valets make good money," Ian said. "You could have been that guy Charlene married."

"But I'm not looking to get married," Vince said with a grin. "Besides, I do make good money, but my mother's staying at a special-care facility, and I have to pay for that. I don't have any brothers or sisters, and it's up to me to take care of my mom—I don't have extra money lying around to support an expensive wife."

"Did Charlene know that when you two were together?"

Vince nodded. "It was one of the first things I told her. I don't think she minded, but she didn't see me as a potential husband either—we just had a good time together."

"And that lasted for how long?"

"About six months or so, on and off. We were never exclusive, and whenever a rich tourist that fit Charlene's bill showed up, she would go out with him. Of course, those things never lasted."

"It sounds like you two were a good match," Ian said. "You were both just looking to have fun—then why end things?"

Vince shrugged. "I guess, maybe we got sick of it after a while? I decided I wanted to meet someone I could have an exclusive relationship with. I never really dated other girls when I was with Charlene, even though she dated other men. She was happy to end things too, said it was hard to explain to guys if I called her the middle of the night."

"That makes sense," I said. "There's only so long you can keep up a relationship like you and Charlene had, especially if you wanted to have an exclusive girlfriend, and Charlene wanted to find a potential husband."

"Yeah," said Ian. "Charlene probably thought she couldn't honestly tell a guy she'd just met that she was single, if she was also dating you on the side."

"That's what I also figured," Vince said. "After we broke up, we would wave if we ever saw each other in the casino, but I've always believed in quick, clean break ups—I don't like to stay friends with my exes, or anything like that. I think Charlene felt the same way. So, like I told you earlier, we haven't talked to each other in over a year."

I was a bit disappointed, but I said, "What can you tell us about her friends?"

"She didn't have any."

"None at all?"

"She wasn't a social person, and I think all she wanted to do was find the right guy, get married, and settle down and have kids."

"But she must've hung out with someone on the weekends?"

Vince shrugged. "She and her brother were very close—I went to the funeral, and I saw how shook up he was. Poor guy."

I nodded. "Did you meet Brad's partner, Chris?"

Vince frowned. "I think I saw Chris,

what, maybe once? I'm not sure what their deal is, whether he and Brad are just business partners, or more."

"Didn't Charlene ever tell you?"

"No, I never asked, not outright. She said Chris was Brad's partner, that's all."

"When you two were together, did Charlene ever act strangely in any way?"

Vince shook his head. "Not unless you call trying to get a bunch of money unusual. I mean, she made decent enough money as a waitress, but she wanted to marry a guy for his money—she didn't care about love, that's what she told me. Said she didn't believe in love, that it was all a myth. That marriage was about family and stability, and that meant a guy with money.

"I asked her if she ever thought about winning the lottery, but she said that she'd worked in the pit for long enough to know that gambling doesn't work. And I asked her if she thought about ever starting up a business, or maybe training for a high earning job like being a doctor, or something, but she just laughed. Said she didn't have the brains for it, and the only way she could get some wealth was by marrying into it."

Ian and I asked him the usual questions about whether Charlene had any enemies that he knew of, or anyone who might want to hurt her, but Vince insisted that Charlene couldn't possibly have any enemies, given how she didn't go out much, or do anything dangerous. He hadn't seen her before she died, so he couldn't tell us if she'd acted unusually before her death or not, and though we asked him a few more questions, trying to uncover something that we may have missed earlier, he told us nothing of interest.

Finally, we said goodbye, and headed away.

"What time does your shift start?" Ian said.

"I've got just under an hour," I said. "Maybe we could head into the Treasury and go to the café that's past the pit. We could have a coffee, and think about things."

Ian and I headed inside, but then I saw Billy hovering around the reception area, and on an impulse, I turned on my heel and walked out again. Billy had seen us, but she hadn't made any move to come and talk to us—she'd just watched us warily.

"She's there again," I told Ian. "It starting to unnerve me."

Instead of heading into the Treasury, Ian and I walked away from the Strip, until we got to Jerry's Diner.

Jerry's Diner is a local institution, far away enough from the Strip to be devoid of tourists, yet packed with locals who work nearby. It has a Spanish-style exterior with a tiled roof, and an obligatory large neon sign outside. The inside is old-school, with gleaming white floor tiles and red vinyl booths. It always smells of fried food and coffee, and Ian and I walked past the tables in the middle of the room and over to a booth at the back.

We ordered a mug of coffee each and a plate of pancakes to share. The lunch we'd had earlier with Glenn seemed to have disappeared from my stomach, and when the pancakes arrived, we dug in with gusto.

"It sucks that Vince couldn't tell us

anything new," Ian said, "but maybe if we talk to Mary tomorrow, we'll learn something."

"I'm tempted to agree with Nanna," I said morosely. "I don't think Mary's going to share whatever she knows. Of course, she might change her mind and cooperate. And pigs might fly."

We were just about to talk some more about Mary, and whether we needed to follow up on Charlene's previous room-mates, when a familiar face came into view.

"I saw you in the Treasury," Billy said. "I don't want to bother you."

I looked at her and sighed. I thought that Billy would have gotten bored of chasing after me by now, but she clearly wasn't going to leave me alone.

"You're here now," Ian said.

Billy turned to him and smiled. "I wanted to know if Tiffany's had a chance to think about it." She turned to me again. "It's been over a day since I asked you—would you like me to help you out? I could be really useful for you guys."

"I'm sorry," I said. "I don't need any more people helping me out."

"Are you sure? Have you really thought about it?"

"Yes. And I can't let you tag along with us—you might get into trouble, and I can't be responsible for you."

"If you're just worried about me getting into trouble, you don't need to stress. I can take care of myself, and I would never blame you if something dangerous happened."

I tried a different tack. "I can't pay you. I hardly make any money from my PI work, and I don't even pay Ian."

Doubt flickered in Billy's eyes. "I need a job—I can't work for you for free. But maybe I can work free for a few days, and then you could see how you like having me as an employee?"

I shook my head. "No, I'm short on funds as it is—I can't afford an employee."

"Okay," Billy said. "How about, I work for you for a few days, while I look for a job here? You don't have to pay me for those days. Once I get a job, I won't work for Ian and you—how does that sound? A free employee for maybe a week or two?"

I shook my head. "No, it's not just the money. Too many cooks spoil the broth."

"So you don't want too many people hanging around you?"

"Something like that. The bottom line is, I'd like you to leave me alone now, please. "

"I think I'd be really useful for you at this time," Billy said. "I know you're in danger."

I frowned at her. "What do you mean?"

"I've been following you for a few days now. And there's someone else who's following you, too."

A chill settled on my heart. "Who?"

"It's this older guy. He's tall. Got gray hair and a crooked nose. He's really sneaky—I almost missed him. But he doesn't seem to know that I'm following you."

The description matched Eli's to a T. Ian and I stared at each other, our eyes wide with panic.

"Are you sure about this?" Ian said to Billy.

Billy nodded. "Absolutely sure. I can tell you two know this man."

I looked at Billy and narrowed my eyes. "You work for him, don't you?"

Billy shook her head, and raised her hands placatingly. "No! Never. I don't know who he is, but I told you, I just moved to Vegas. I want to help you guys out. If you're in danger, just let me know, and I'll be there to help you out."

"We're not in danger," I fibbed, forcing my voice to stay steady. "Please, just leave us alone."

"Let me know if you change your mind," Billy said, and I watched as she headed over to a booth a few paces away.

I turned to Ian. "This is not good."

"It's terrible." Ian sounded as scared as I felt. "If Billy is telling the truth…"

"If she's not telling the truth, then it means she knows who Eli is, and the only way she'd know that is if she worked for him."

"But if she worked for him, she wouldn't just come out and tell us something like that."

I nodded. "That doesn't make sense. I'm pretty sure Billy doesn't work for Eli. But in that case…"

"In that case," Ian said, finishing the sentence for me, "Eli must really be following you around."

"Which means that he knows something's up. If Eli knew that Tariq was in Santa Verona, then maybe he found out that he left—and Eli's just put two and two together and figured out that Tariq left Santa Verona to come to Vegas. Which means that Tariq is trying to get in touch with Stone."

"And the easiest way to get in touch with Stone is through you."

I shuddered. "This is not good," I said, repeating myself.

"Maybe Billy's right," Ian said, "maybe we need some help here. Do you think we should ask Nanna to join us?"

"No! Nanna thinks she's tough, but she's really an eighty-year-old woman who just wants to have some fun. I wouldn't ever get her mixed up in this kind of thing."

"Then maybe you should let Stone know about this."

I nodded. "I'll do that. As soon as I get home, I'll use that special phone Stone gave me for getting in touch with him, and send him a text about this. He might have some ideas."

"In the meantime," Ian said, "we should be extra careful."

CHAPTER 13

The next morning, I went over to Ian's for breakfast, for a change. It turned out that Tariq had gone through Ian's kitchen cabinets, and found flour and a couple of other baking ingredients, and made us muffins for breakfast.

The three of us sat around and had a delicious breakfast of chocolate and blueberry muffins, while Snowflake watched us carefully from the countertop.

We talked a bit about how Tariq was settling in, and he insisted that he wasn't bored and was fine with staying inside. I had texted Stone the night before to let him know about Eli's potentially watching us, and Stone had sent a terse response—"Stay safe, tell Tariq. I'll keep an eye on you guys."

So I took Stone's advice, and filled Tariq in on the Eli situation.

He didn't say anything, but his eyes grew stony and hard.

"I wish I could come out to help you," he said.

Ian and I quickly shook our heads. "It would be more dangerous if you came out —at least now, Eli doesn't know for sure that you're here, or that you've got anything to do with us."

Tariq nodded. "What are you two going to do today?"

Just then, Ian's phone buzzed with a text. "It's Nanna," he said after reading it, "she's on her way over here, and she wants to talk to us."

We said a hasty goodbye to Tariq, and headed back to my apartment. Nanna showed up a few minutes later.

She was dressed in black sweatpants, and a black T-shirt.

"Let's do it!" she said, as soon as she entered the apartment.

"Do what?" I eyed her warily. Wearing all black was Nanna's idea of what a "break in" costume should comprise of.

"We're going to explore Mary's apartment, of course."

I shook my head. "I hate to keep saying no, but you do realize that it's illegal to break in?"

"You know that she's hiding the truth from you, and you know that you've got to find out the truth," Nanna said evenly. "How else do you intend to learn what's really going on?"

"We don't have to break in," Ian said, "but let's at least go there, and see if she'll talk to us."

"You know she'll have work right now," I argued.

"Then let's see if Christine knows anything about what's going on."

I couldn't dissuade Ian and Nanna, so the three of us drove over to Mary's apartment, and as we headed upstairs, I peered along the street. I couldn't see anyone following us—neither Billy nor Eli—so maybe we were safe for now. Maybe Eli had followed us once or twice, and he'd given up again; maybe Billy would change her mind about trying to "help,", too.

We knocked loudly on the door, but there was no response.

"Seems like nobody's home," Ian said.

"Maybe Christine's inside, and she's asleep," I said.

"Maybe she's inside, and something's wrong," Nanna said. "Don't you want to go and make sure she's okay?"

"The longer we stand out here," Ian said, "the more suspicious we look. I vote for breaking in, and we should do it right now."

I shook my head. "I think we should just wait to talk to Christine."

"I'm not going to stand out here any longer," Nanna announced. "I've got my own set of lock picks, and I found a nice website on the Internet, where they explained how to do this. Stand back!"

"I really don't think—" I stopped talking when I saw a man coming up the stairs.

Nanna had already inserted a lock pick, and she was jiggling away furiously. She

LUCKY CHARM IN LAS VEGAS

looked as suspicious as an eighty-year-old woman with a lock pick could.

Ian and I quickly stood on either side of her, all the better to hide her lock picks.

"Hurry up," Ian hissed. "What if we get caught?"

"I can't get the lock pick out," Nanna stage-whispered back. "Otherwise I'd just move away—maybe I'll look like my key's stuck."

I was starting to panic, when the door creaked open, and Nanna gave a low, triumphant whoop. "I knew I could do it! You can learn anything from the Internet."

"That doesn't mean you have to learn everything they teach you on random websites," I grumbled, as Ian, Nanna and I all rushed in. Nanna remembered to pull out her lock pick set, and we closed the door safely behind us.

"Hello…" I called out as soon as we were inside. "Christine? Are you in here?"

But there was no answer.

"Maybe she's still at work," Ian said. "She might walk in any minute now."

I looked at my watch. It was almost lunch time, and I knew Ian was right.

"Or Mary could come home from work," Nanna said. "One of us should stand guard."

"Maybe Tiffany should go," Ian suggested. "You can let us know if someone shows up."

"I'm not going," I said. "I don't approve of doing this, but now that we're in here, I need to make sure everything's okay."

"I'm not going out," Nanna said. "You two wouldn't even be in here if it wasn't for me."

"I think we should toss a coin," Ian said, "and then Nanna and me can decide who should be outside."

Nanna picked heads, and Ian picked tails, and then they flipped the coin. Heads came up.

Ian and I looked at Nanna expectantly.

"I'm not going out," Nanna declared. "It's hot, and I'm old. You know the heat's bad for me. Plus, an old lady standing outside in the heat looks suspicious. But a young man standing outside, and pretending to talk on his cell phone looks absolutely normal."

"Nanna's right," I admitted reluctantly. "We can't have her standing outside in the heat. Ian, I don't think you should be out in this heat either—maybe you can wait in the car, and then if you see either Mary or Christine, you can give us a call."

Ian grumbled, but he made his way out, and promised to let us know if any of the roommates showed up.

Nanna and I put on gloves, wiped down the door knob, and then made our way through the apartment.

There was quite a lot to go through— the living room we were in, the kitchen area, a small dining area, and then three bedrooms. There was also a bathroom that looked like it hadn't been cleaned often enough, with old fittings and a dripping tap.

It was easy to tell which one Charlene's room had been—that was the one with no covers on the bed, and nothing in the wardrobe.

We glanced quickly at the two other

bedrooms, and then decided to start with the room that had a wardrobe full of black clothes.

"I'm sure the other one's Christine's room," I said. "Might as well start here."

"And then, if we've got time, we can go through Christine's room, too."

I hated to agree with Nanna, but she had a point—we'd gone through all this trouble to make our way in, so we might as well look through everything we could.

Nanna and I looked through Mary's bedroom slowly and carefully, but nothing jumped out at us. Next, we went through the bathroom, and then the kitchen, living room, and dining room. Finally, we looked through Christine's bedroom. And then, just to be extra careful, we looked through the room that used to be Charlene's, even though everything had been removed, and only a bed, mattress, and empty wardrobe stood there.

We were just about to head out, when Ian called, and said, in an urgent, hushed voice, "I just saw Mary! She's on her way up."

"Nanna and I'll get out," I said. "We'll pretend we came to see her."

I hung up, and Nanna and I quickly made our way outside, locking the door carefully behind us, and shoving our gloves into our handbags.

Mary noticed us when she was a few paces away from her door.

She narrowed her eyes at me. "What are you doing here? And who's this old woman?"

She chucked her head toward Nanna, and Nanna bristled. "Who are you calling old?"

"You! Don't you ever look in the mirror?"

"I prefer the term 'wise,'" Nanna said haughtily. "Just because I've got white hair, it doesn't make me old. Age is a number, and I'm young inside."

Mary rolled her eyes. "Whatever. Where's that funny-looking partner of yours, the one with the curly red hair?"

"I'm not funny-looking," Ian said from behind Mary. "I was just parking the car."

"Well, whatever," Mary said. "What are you all doing here?"

"We came to talk to you," Nanna said. "You were Charlene's roommate after all."

"I've already told you everything I can," Mary said. "I don't have to talk to you. You're not the police."

I raised one eyebrow at her. "Did the police come around here?"

Mary nodded. "Yeah, right after Charlene died."

"We really would appreciate some of your time," Ian said politely. "We think you might be able to help us."

"How?"

"There's something you're not telling us," I said. "We're here to see if you can remember anything new."

"Well, I can't."

"We know you went to a pawn shop last night, and that it's related to Charlene's death."

Mary looked at me with alarm in her eyes. "What? How do you know that?"

I shrugged. "We have our ways."

Mary took a deep breath and recovered.

"Yeah? So what if I went to a pawn shop, there's nothing wrong with that. Doesn't mean it's related to her death at all."

"I think the cops would be interested to know that you're selling your roommate's stuff. The bags and jewelry weren't yours."

Mary's eyes widened again, glittering with panic. "How do you know that?"

"Like I said, we've got our ways."

Mary looked over her shoulder, and then opened the door. "You'd better come in."

When we were all settled down in her living room, Mary said, "You're not going to tell anyone, are you?"

"Maybe Christine should know."

"Why would Christine want to know about Charlene's stuff? It's nothing to her."

I raised my eyebrows. I'd taken a shot in the dark, thinking that Mary had been stealing Christine's things as well, but clearly I was wrong. "How did you get your hands on Charlene's things?"

Mary shrugged. "I used to borrow her stuff all the time, when she was alive. She never minded."

Nanna said, "Did Charlene know that you 'borrowed' her things?"

Mary shrugged. "She wouldn't have cared. She had so many nice things and she hardly ever used them. They're not my taste, but I've got a girlfriend who likes those kind of things, and she liked to carry the designer bags whenever she went out to have some fun—said she got more free drinks and better treatment that way. I always gave everything back within a day or two."

"Except when you didn't," I said.

Mary rolled her eyes. "Charlene's dead, and I know designer bags and jewelry are expensive. There wasn't anything in them, and it's not like the police had any use for them, and what would her family do with them either?"

"So you stole them," Ian said.

Mary smiled. "I gave them better homes. I wasn't actually sure what I was going to do—as soon as I heard she was dead, I knew the cops would stop by and take everything. I've watched enough TV shows to know that's how they work. So I headed into her room, and gathered up everything I thought might come in handy."

"What were you going to do with them?"

"At first I thought I'd sell them online, but then I didn't want a paper trail, or an Internet trail. I was going to ask my girl-friend if she wanted anything, but then I worried that maybe she would tell someone about it. I was still deciding what to do when you guys came around to talk—and then I thought, what if you wanted to go through my things, or something."

"So you panicked," Nanna said, "and you took them to the pawn shop, and you got some good money for them."

"I wouldn't say good money," Mary said. "Those places are rip-offs."

"But maybe they could have come in handy during the investigation," I said. "Did you ever think of that?"

Mary laughed. "A couple of designer handbags? It's not like they're great big clues or anything, and I could use the money. Living here is expensive."

"Did you sell any of Charlene's things when she was alive?"

Mary shook her head quickly. "No, of course not. She would've found out in the end."

"How much did you get for selling everything last night?"

"A couple of grand."

"Maybe you killed her," Nanna said. "Maybe you thought you could kill her, sell all her things and get a decent amount of money."

Mary shook her head quickly. "No, of course not. I would never do something like that. Besides, who kills someone over a couple of grand?"

Ian and I exchanged a glance. That was true. Unless they were a drug addict, most people wouldn't just kill their roommate to get their hands on a few designer bags. Besides, Mary had clearly been unsure of what to do with her loot, waiting 'til the very last minute before she headed over to a pawnshop.

"That doesn't mean you should sell off a dead person's things," Nanna said.

"Whatever, old lady," Mary said. "I'm just trying to survive here, and it's a—what d'ya call it?—it's a victimless crime. No one got hurt."

I glanced off into the distance, and tried to judge whether that was true. But Mary seemed to be telling the truth, and I couldn't imagine her mustering up the ability to stab Charlene to death. I'd seen the photos the CSI team had taken, and they were gruesome.

"Are you done now?" Mary said. "I'd like to have a shower and then go out for a bit."

I looked over at her, remembering the way her eyes had flickered when I'd mentioned Chris's name. "There's something you're not telling us about Chris."

Mary sighed. "I suppose I should have just told you the first time."

"Don't tell me you're having an affair with him or something."

Mary laughed. "Chris? No, I'm pretty sure he's gay. I think he and Brad are together."

"So you've met him."

"I wouldn't say that."

"Why don't you start from the beginning? What do you know about Chris, and
how did you find out?"

"I don't exactly *know* anything," Mary
said, gulping nervously. "But one day,
Charlene was home, and she thought I was
out. I was actually in my room, taking a
nap, but then I woke up because I heard a
crash. Charlene was arguing with a man,
and she called him Chris. I don't know if it
was a different Chris or not, but I don't
think so, because they were talking
about Brad."

"What do you remember?"

"Well, I woke up to the crash, and then I
heard their voices, but I couldn't make out
what they were saying. The only thing I
could hear clearly was when the man, Chris
or whoever, said, 'Stop it! I don't want you
creating trouble like this.' And then Charlene said, 'I won't. I'm not going to keep this
a secret. I'm going to tell everyone—it's
what's best for my brother in the long run.'"

Ian and I exchanged a glance. I was
about to say something, when Mary
went on.

"And then Chris said, 'It's not what's best, and you'd better stop with this sorta talk.' After that, their voices died down again, and I couldn't hear what else they were talking about. But it sounded to me like Chris and Brad must've been together, and Charlene was threatening to tell everyone, and maybe Chris or Brad, either one of them, wasn't ready to come out of the closet yet. Something like that."

I nodded. "What happened after that?"

"Nothing," Mary said. "I gave them a couple of minutes, and then I heard the front door closing. I figured that Chris must've left. I stayed in my room for a few more minutes, but I couldn't hear anything else, so I fell asleep again."

"Did you ask Charlene about it later?" Nanna said.

Mary looked at her, and shook her head. "No, I thought it was none of my business. And I think Chris may have said something like that too, that it was none of Charlene's business, but I can't remember exactly."

"What about Brad?" Ian said. "Did you see him around?"

Mary nodded. "He'd come around to chat with Charlene sometimes, so I'd see him every now and then."

"Did you ever hear him talking about Chris?"

Mary shook her head. "Not really. I mean, sometimes I'd hear Charlene asking Brad how Chris was doing, and Brad would say 'okay.' But nothing more than that. Hang on—now that I think about it, one time, I was in the bathroom, and I overheard Charlene telling Brad that Chris was being mean to her, and telling her to mind her own business. I thought Brad would say something nasty about Chris—I know he and Charlene were close. But he said, what Chris said was important, and that Chris was important to him, and that Charlene should mind her own business."

"Why didn't you tell us this sooner?" I said, annoyed that we'd overlooked something which could potentially be important. "Did you tell the cops?"

"No," Mary said, looking sheepish. "I guess I should go tell them now. But I don't

want to have too much to do with the cops.
They make me nervous."

"Because you've nicked things from
here and there before," Nanna said sagely.
"You probably keep moving around from
one apartment to another before you get
caught."

Mary's eyes flicked over to Nanna, but
she ignored the comment and looked back
at us. "I'd forgotten that Brad had defended
Chris to Charlene once. That's a bit strange,
since Brad adored Charlene—I suppose it
means that Chris really was important
to him."

I nodded. "Yes, whatever it is, we'd
better look into it. Is there anything else
you can remember about Chris and Brad,
or anything about Charlene?"

She shook her head. "No, I've told you
everything I can think of."

We stayed there a few more minutes,
hoping that Mary would remember something more, but she didn't, and told us that
this time, she'd really told us everything
she knew.

Finally, the three of us left her apartment, and headed back to my car. I looked over my shoulder both ways, but I couldn't see anyone watching us.

When we were all in the car, Ian said, "I believe Mary. I think she's told us everything she knows, and I don't think she's lying this time."

"Me neither," Nanna said. "It's a good thing she remembered about Chris and Brad."

I nodded. "I'm not sure how useful this information is, but maybe we can try to talk to Chris and Brad again. Funny how their names always seem to come up together—maybe they'll change their minds and decide to talk to us."

"Where do they live?" Nanna said. "Maybe we can break into their apartment, too."

"They live in separate apartments," I said. "I looked up their addresses. And no, we're not breaking in to any more places."

"We'll see about that," Nanna said. "And don't even think about telling Wes what we've been up to."

"I wouldn't dream of it," I said with a

laugh. "Wes would tell Mom and Dad, and then I'd be the one in who's in trouble for letting you get into all this."

"At least you've learned something new," Nanna said. "And probably this is something important. We should definitely break into Chris's place, too."

CHAPTER 14

*N*anna, Ian and I argued during the short drive home, and all through our lunch of reheated frozen pizza. The argument didn't stop even after the pizza disappeared, and we kept going round in circles.

Nanna was insistent that Brad and Chris wouldn't want to talk to us, and that we definitely needed to break in to their apartments. Ian was undecided, but I was worried that Nanna was getting some kind of "break-in fever."

"I'm not going to let you do it again," I kept saying. "Just because you've gotten away with this once today doesn't mean you will again."

"But Brad and Chris have already refused to tell you anything," Nanna said. "We need to be sneaky."

"But I don't want to do anything like breaking in again."

"Ian knows I'm right," Nanna said, turning to Ian. "Right, Ian?"

Ian shrugged, and then his face brightened. "I know! We don't have to break-in. But Nanna's right, I don't think they're going to want to talk to us. How about if we just do some surveillance, without actually talking to them?"

"We did get useful information from doing surveillance on Mary," I agreed. "Maybe being sneaky and surveilling them is the way to go."

Nanna let out a disappointed grunt. "But I'm not going to be around when you guys do your surveillance! I need to get home soon, and I know that Ian wants to do surveillance at night while you're off at your shift. And I can't sit in a car all day; I need to go to the bathroom more often these days."

"We can do some surveillance now," I suggested.

"Even better!" Ian said. "How about we go to the laundromat, and hang out there?"

"But they'll recognize us," Nanna said. "Of course, they've never seen me before."

"Tiffany and I can wear disguises," Ian told Nanna. "You don't need to wear one, because you're right, they didn't see you earlier."

Nanna crossed her arms over her chest. "If you two are wearing disguises, I'll be wearing one, too!"

Ian looked at me, and we smiled at each other. At least Nanna had given up her idea of breaking into Brad or Chris's apartment.

"I'll head into my apartment and get the disguises," Ian said.

"Why don't we just go over to your place and put on wigs and stuff in there?" Nanna said.

Ian and I exchanged a panicked look.

"Uh…" I said.

Ian was quicker with the excuse than me. "Snowflake's trashed the place," he said. "And she's getting into an excitable mood these days. I think if we had visitors, she wouldn't even let us get dressed, and we really need to get going soon, if we want to see them at the laundromat. I don't know how long they'll be working there."

"But Snowflake always seems so gentle," Nanna protested.

"It's something to do with hormones," Ian said. "The vet said to just give her a few days to calm down."

Nanna seemed satisfied by that explanation, and a few minutes later, Ian was back with wigs, glasses, and scarves.

I pulled a blond wig over my brown hair, and picked a pair of thick-rimmed glasses that made me look like a nerdy computer programmer. Ian went with a bald wig that he'd worn before—I joked that it made him look like a fat Bruce Willis, but he was insistent that it made him look handsome. Nanna decided to go with a scarf wrapped around her head, something that I thought didn't make her look too different, but I didn't say so aloud.

Once we were suitably dressed, I

grabbed a bag of dirty laundry, and we headed over to the laundromat.

It was early afternoon by the time we drove up to Sunset Laundry, and the laundromat looked empty. One lonely clothes dryer was running. I read the instructions and tossed my clothes into a washing machine.

Chris was sitting at the table today, and I couldn't see Brad anywhere.

Once the wash cycle had started, Ian, Nanna and I all went over to the bench to wait.

"There's a bar next door," Chris said helpfully. He didn't seem to like us sitting there, and he went on, "There's also a Mexican place, and a café a few blocks down that serves fantastic coffee. It'll take a couple of hours for your clothes to all be done. You can come back in an hour to shift it to the dryer."

"Let's go to the bar," Nanna said, just as Ian said, "Let's go to the Mexican place!"

I glanced from Ian to Nanna. And then, I looked at Chris, who was watching us suspiciously.

"We can't wait in here," I said out loud, trying to allay Chris's suspicions. "Let's go outside and have a chat about where we should go."

The three of us headed out, and then we stood on the sidewalk in front of the window, and pretended to talk animatedly.

"The bar!" Nanna said, pointing her finger at the bar.

Ian shook his head vigorously. "No, the Mexican place that!"

"We need to keep an eye on this place," I said in a low voice. "If we go somewhere, we won't be able to do that. How about, we get into my car, and I'll go for a one-minute drive, and then we can come back and park here? Chris will think we've gone off to run some errands or something like that."

The others agreed that it was a good idea, and we did just that. I wondered if anything would come of the surveillance— if we learned nothing new, Nanna would be trying to convince us to break into Brad or Chris's apartment again.

But I had just finished parking my car again, when we saw a short, stocky man with tattoos up both arms walking into the laundromat carrying a duffel bag.

"I wonder if I could go out and see if the man's just here to do laundry," Ian said. "I could pretend to be checking on the washing."

"Ian's right—if we don't go in, we'll never know what's happening," Nanna said. "We could pretend we're paranoid about our clothes."

There was a brief disagreement over who would get to go and check on the laundry, and in the end, the three of us all trooped back to the laundromat. But when we were at the door, I peered in through the window, and there were no signs of Chris or the other man. The three of us stood outside hesitantly for a few seconds.

"I'll sneak in alone," I said. "I noticed a door the other day, and I guess it leads to an office. If neither of them are in the laundromat, they're probably having a conversation in there."

I knew Ian and Nanna both wanted to come with me, but for once, they were actually logical, and understood that three people would make more noise than one.

I crept inside, trying to be as silent as I could. The door I'd seen earlier was closed, and I slowly made my way over, and wrapped my fingers around the door knob.

I paused for a second, and took a deep breath.

If I opened the door, it might creak loudly. I pressed my ear against the door, but I couldn't hear anything—they must've been talking in very low voices. Crossing my fingers, I turned the knob very, very slowly. So far, no sound.

I pushed the door open a crack, and waited.

"Fifty thousand," a man's voice was saying. I'd never heard that voice before, so I assumed it was the man we'd seen walking in.

I waited for a few seconds, wondering if either of them had noticed the door open-ing. But neither of them commented on it, so I simply froze in place and hoped they wouldn't sense my presence.

There were a few long seconds of

silence, and then Chris's voice said, "Yep, that's all of it."

The other voice growled, "You know what to do. The usual."

"Don't worry," Chris said, "tell your boss it'll all be done as soon as I can. I'll make the deposit, and then after we've spent a bit, we'll do the transfer."

The other man grunted, and muttered something I couldn't hear. "I'll see you again soon," I heard Chris say, and I took that as my cue to leave.

I snuck outside as silently as I'd come in. Once I was standing in the parking lot in the bright sunlight, I let my breath out in a loud whoosh. I hadn't even realized I'd stopped breathing.

Ian and Nanna came over eagerly to join me, and we all stood outside near where I'd parked my car, until we saw the tattooed man get into a white Prius and drive off.

"What happened?" Ian said.

My hands felt sweaty, and I looked around. I couldn't see Chris anywhere, but I felt as though I was being watched.

"Do you see anyone?" I asked. "I feel like someone's watching us"

"I certainly feel like I'm being watched," Nanna declared. "But maybe it's that other guy, Brad. The one who's Charlene's brother."

Ian and I exchanged a glance.

"I don't think so," I said cautiously. "It might be someone else."

"Who else?"

But I didn't feel like telling her about Eli or Billy, so instead, I said, "Let's head back to my apartment and I can tell you what I've learned."

"But what about the clothes?"

"You're right," I said with a sigh. "They should be done in a few minutes—we can transfer them to the dryer, and when that's done, we can wait in my car, and I can tell you what I heard."

Once the clothes were in the dryer and the three of us had gotten back in my car, I filled Ian and Nanna in on the conversation I'd overheard.

"It sounds like money laundering to me," Nanna said, once I'd finished telling them what I'd heard. "The man with the duffel must've been carrying a lot of cash on himself."

"I think it's money laundering too," Ian said. "I once saw a movie that featured a mafia dude laundering money, and after that, I looked up how to do it. Not that I would ever do it myself. Of course, now I've forgotten how exactly you get it to work. How does it work?" he asked, turning to Nanna.

"You need an illegal source of money first," Nanna said. "That's why money laundering is so bad—it's only criminals who do it."

"But why wouldn't you just spend the money you've got? Why launder it?"

"Sometimes criminals want to legalize their money, so they can do legitimate things with it—like open a legitimate business, or buy a house, or get a loan from the bank. So they can't just go around with cash all the time. They need to show a source of income."

"So that's where gambling or a laundromat comes in?"

"Exactly. Once you've got the cash, you need some way to make it legal."

"So let's say I am a criminal," Ian said. "And I've got one million dollars I want to want launder. What do I do?"

"I'll tell you what I think the laundromat is doing," Nanna said. "They're taking cash from someone, and then they'll pretend that they earned that money through the laundromat. It's a cash business, so all they have to do is deposit into the bank and say they earned it from the laundromat. If they're doing this on someone else's behalf, then they probably take a cut for themselves, and transfer the money to the guy who's laundering."

"I noticed another name when I was looking up the laundromat," I said. "It was some kind of corporation. I didn't pay it much attention, because I just assumed that Chris and Brad had started the laundromat as partners, but then they'd later decided to limit their liability and put it under a corporation as well. Maybe I should go and have a look—maybe the corporation isn't just about the two of them."

"Maybe not," Nanna said. "You can't launder money unless you're in the business, or a part of the business, that you're laundering money from. If there's someone else involved in the corporation, then that person must be the one who's doing the laundering. And chances are, this person isn't some kind of honest businessmen—they've got a criminal enterprise that they're trying to hide."

"And if they are a criminal," Ian said slowly, "they're more likely to be involved in things like murders. Maybe this other person knows something about Charlene's death."

CHAPTER 15

*W*e dropped Nanna home, and then Ian and I headed back to my apartment to research the laundromat. I fired up my private investigator's database, and then I went over to a website that researched businesses, and then back to my database. Cross-referencing different kinds of information finally gave me what I was looking for.

The laundromat was owned by Brad, Chris, and the Brad and Chris Corporation.

I'd assumed that the Brad and Chris Corporation was just some corporation that the two men had set up for themselves, but when I dug into it, I found that it was owned by another company, which in turn was owned by someone else, which was partially owned by another entity. The final owner turned out to be a man named George Dragovich.

Unfortunately, there was very little publicly available information about him.

A combination of news articles, and information from my database turned up that George was known by his friends as "Drago," and was a terrible, horrible, no good scoundrel.

George—or Drago—was involved in all manner of illegal activities, and had been investigated by the police a few times, but with no luck on the authorities' part. He was involved in a complex operation that kept him protected, the way a mafia godfather was protected by his complicated "organizational" structure and his loyal, terrified minions. The rumors I'd uncovered implicated Drago's involvement in everything from racketeering to prostitution to drugs.

It took us a few hours to dig up all the

information, and by then, it was time for my shift.

"This isn't what I expected to find out," I told Ian. "If Chris and Brad were involved with Drago, then maybe Charlene was involved as well."

"It doesn't sound like Charlene had anything to do with the laundromat," Ian said. "Do you think she even knew they were involved in laundering money for Drago?"

"I'm not sure, but then again, I never expected to find a hardcore criminal involved in this murder. I'd thought that it would be a rather open and shut case—that maybe she'd been killed by a boyfriend, or a former boyfriend had gotten jealous of Andrew. If this man Drago is involved…"

"This is too big for us. We need to go to the police with our information, and maybe they can help us out."

I nodded. "I can't do anything more tonight, because I have to head in to work, but first thing tomorrow morning, we'll go see Ryan. Maybe he can tell us something, or he can go investigate Drago himself. I'm sure the cops will be interested to know that a criminal organization could be involved with Charlene's death."

CHAPTER 16

My shift passed rather quickly. I was more distracted than usual, but I still appreciated being in the pit after a long day of investigating people who had turned out to be criminals. Investigating is rewarding, since my investigations often help people uncover the truth, but it doesn't pay all that well, and work can be irregular and unpredictable. Working in the pit is the opposite of working as an investigator.

The casino pit is like a familiar second home to me—I've gotten used to the bright lights and noises of the gambling area, just like people get used to living in a particular neighborhood. There was a time when I'd hoped to quit my job. But when I'd actually been forced to make a choice, I'd come to appreciate everything that this job provides me—a steady paycheck, and a chance to unwind.

Sure, there are seedy elements to every casino—but nothing like the dangerous criminal we'd uncovered during this investigation. Drago was rumored to have been involved in the gruesome death of a drug kingpin who was trying to encroach on his territory; I tried to push the details of what I'd read out of my mind, but it was clear that Drago was cruel and sadistic and had intended to send a message to his criminal competition with that death.

I was certain that Drago was involved in Charlene's death in one way or another.

Before I knew it, my shift was over, and I met with Ian and walked back home with him. I glanced over my shoulder every now and then, but I couldn't make out anyone following us—either Billy, or Eli or one of his men. Occasionally, I thought I heard footsteps, but when I turned around, there was no one.

~

The next morning, Ian came over for breakfast, but once again, he'd left Snowflake in his apartment.

"I baked white chocolate and raspberry muffins," he said, placing the box on my countertop. "I thought we should take something for Elwood, just in case we run into him again on a different investigation. Do you think we should take some for Ryan as well?"

"That would be a good idea. Although, this information we're about to share with him should be gift enough," I grumbled.

"He might not think that way," Ian said, as we each settled down with a muffin and a mug of coffee. "I researched Drago some more after you went to work, and there are all kinds of rumors about him, but nobody's ever proved anything."

"That just shows how dangerous and clever he is. It's only the stupid criminals who get caught."

We chewed our food thoughtfully, and then I said, "How is Tariq doing?"

"He helped me with these muffins. He says cooking and baking helps him to relax, and that he had to depend on his own skills for food for a long time. He's really getting along with Snowflake—she's always happy to play with him."

"He seems nice, but I'll be glad when he and Stone have left for DC."

"When do you think that will be?"

"I'm not sure. I think Stone is still trying to set some meetings up. It's difficult, because Johnson has to convince people to have an unofficial meeting first, otherwise, they'd just arrest Stone on the spot."

"He'll figure out something. Eli might have powerful contacts, but I'm sure Johnson has more than a few of his own."

CHAPTER 17

*B*y the time we showed up at the precinct, it was late morning, and we headed over to Elwood's desk first.

When he saw the box of muffins we'd brought for him, his eyes glittered and he just about drooled.

"I knew I could count on you guys!" he said. "Next time you need any information, you come straight to me—that boyfriend of yours is pretty useless."

I laughed. "I don't think he's useless, but I'm glad you're happy with the muffins."

"I'm going to make more time for baking," Ian promised. "And every time I bake something new, I'll bring a box for you."

Elwood beamed at us, and then we made our way over Ryan's desk. For once, we found him doing paperwork instead of being out on a case, and he looked up and grinned when we approached.

"I was hoping for an excuse to take a break," he said, drawing me in for a quick kiss. "Is that box for me?"

I nodded. "We could only save two for you, but I hope you like them."

Ryan looked at Ian. "I know I've got you to thank for this—Tiffany never seems to have any time for baking or cooking."

Ian beamed. "That's okay, the more I bake, the more I enjoy it. Mixing every-thing together is pretty relaxing, and the smells when you put something in the oven—mmmm."

Ryan locked the box of muffins away in his desk drawer, and then he turned to us again. "I'm guessing this isn't a purely social visit?"

I shook my head. "Could we talk some-where private?"

Ryan raised an eyebrow at me. "More

questions? You know I've told you every-thing I can."

"It's not that. We're here to share some information, not take it."

"That's a first." Ryan smiled at me, teas-ing, but he led us over to the friendly conference room with its couches and fake potted plant. Once the door was closed behind us, he said, "So, what have you guys found out?"

"Have you looked into the laundromat?"

"Just briefly—we're not really interested in it. The only connection to Charlene's death is that Brad and Chris own the place."

I shook my head. "It's not just Brad and Chris, it's also owned by the Brad and Chris Corporation."

Ryan looked a bit confused. "Isn't that what I just said?"

I shook my head again. "No, the Brad and Chris Corporation isn't owned by Brad and Chris—it's a shell company owned by George Dragovich."

Ryan's eyes widened at the name, and he leaned back and crossed his arms. "Are you sure about this?"

I tilted my chin up. "Of course I am! We're always thorough in our research." Unlike the police, I wanted to add, but I didn't. I was the spitting image of tact.

Ryan sighed and leaned forward again, clasping his hands together. "This is surprising information, but I'm not sure that it's connected to Charlene's death."

"You don't think that a known criminal working together with Charlene's brother and his partner has anything to do with her death?"

Ryan shook his head. "There are such things as coincidences, you know."

"Not in an open murder investigation," I argued. "You have to at least look into this."

"There were never any indications that Charlene knew Drago or ever met him."

"But you never specifically asked about it."

Ryan shrugged. "I can show his photo around to everyone, and ask Brad and Chris—but even if Charlene had met Drago once or twice, what difference does that make? He's never been involved with her or anything."

"But you don't know that," I countered. "You've never actually asked."

Ryan leaned back, and rubbed a hand across his forehead. "You're right. I can't just write it off—I'll go and have a word about this. Though I think the whole thing is just a coincidence, Drago is a dangerous man when it comes to other criminals, or his criminal enterprises, but I can't see why he would be involved in the death of a cocktail waitress."

"So you're not really going to investigate Drago," I muttered under my breath, unable to keep the disappointment off my face.

I don't think Ryan heard what I'd said, but Ian was sitting next to me, and he definitely had.

Ian said, "If the cops won't investigate Drago properly, maybe Tiffany and I should."

Ryan's eyes flashed, and he held out one hand. "Woah! Stop. There is no way I can have you talking to a dangerous criminal like Drago. If he thinks you two are out to take him down, or hurt his income streams in any way, he won't hesitate to take you down. We've never gotten any proof on the guy, but we're fairly sure that murder is not something that's new to him."

"So he wouldn't think twice about killing someone," I countered, "even if that someone is a cocktail waitress, and not a criminal. How can you even be sure that Charlene wasn't involved in something criminal? Maybe she was running drugs for Drago."

Ryan smiled. "You're grasping at straws. We investigated Charlene properly, and she never had anything to do with drugs or anything illegal at all. If anything, maybe we should turn this information about the laundromat over to the IRS, so that they can investigate Chris and Brad—those two are probably involved in money laundering or something like that."

"That's what we think," I muttered, unable to stop feeling disappointed that Ryan hadn't been as enthusiastic about this information as I'd hoped.

"I'll look into Drago," Ryan promised. "But I don't want you to get your hopes up. We can't investigate him outright, or he'll get suspicious, and it's highly unlikely that he ever had anything to do with Charlene."

"Maybe Tiffany and I can still investigate," Ian said. "We can be subtle about it."

Ryan turned to Ian and grinned. "I've never known you to be subtle about anything."

"Ok," said Ian. "But I can try."

Ryan and I both laughed at that, and Ian looked at us, puzzled. But then Ryan sobered up and looked at me seriously. "I'm not kidding about this—Drago is a very dangerous man. I can't risk you getting hurt by trying to investigate him. More than anything, I want you to be safe. Which means you and Ian need to stay away from Drago."

$\mathcal{A}$s we drove back to my apartment, I didn't know how to feel about our conversation with Ryan.

On the one hand, it was nice of him to be concerned about my safety. On the other hand, I didn't like someone telling me how to run my investigation. And while I understood the need for the cops' discretion in investigating Drago, I wasn't sure there needed to be so much pussyfooting around the issue of whether or not Drago could be involved in Charlene's death.

Once Ian and I were back in my apartment, we decided that since we weren't getting anywhere with Drago, we'd look up the details of Charlene's former roommates and try to get in touch with them. The private investigator's database and the Internet turned up nothing of interest, and two of them didn't answer their phones. The other roommate told us that she'd moved to Florida, and the fourth agreed to meet us the next day.

"It's a long shot," I told Ian, "but we've got to keep trying. Maybe one of them had something to do with Charlene's death after all."

"We need to be thorough," Ian agreed, "even though we think that this Drago guy is the one who's involved. I couldn't find a phone number for Drago on the Internet— I guess you've got something from your database?"

I nodded. "I got his office address and a phone number, but I'm sure it's not one that he'll answer personally. We'll probably get the runaround from some assistant."

"We can always turn up at the office."

I was thinking about that, when there was a sharp knock on my door.

"Maybe it's Tariq," Ian suggested, as I got up to open the door.

When I opened the door, I found myself staring at a slouching man wearing a bright Hawaiian-print shirt and khaki shorts. He had scraggly blond hair that fell past his shoulders, and an equally scraggly blond mustache. A baseball cap was jammed onto his head, and shiny white touristy sneakers adorned his feet.

It was only when he removed the cap and the blond wig that I grinned. "Stone! Your disguise is as ugly as any of Ian's."

His lips quirked up and once he'd stepped inside, Ian said, "I'll go get Tariq. I assume you're here to see him?"

Stone nodded, and Ian left for his apartment.

Stone settled down on one corner of the couch, and watched me as I perched nervously on the edge of a chair. I felt slightly awkward, and didn't know what to say. Stone was always very quiet, but for once, he was the one who started the conversation.

"I've been trying to keep an eye on you. I'm sure Eli suspects Tariq is here, and that you know something about it."

"Then why doesn't he come over to my apartment to try to talk to me?"

"Because he's sure you'll lie to protect me."

That wasn't very reassuring, but I said, "Should you even be keeping an eye out? That sounds dangerous."

Stone shook his head. "I think it's time for me to stop hiding. I need to take risks—if Eli wants to have a confrontation, he can have it."

I chewed my lip thoughtfully. Was it really a good idea to confront a man like Eli? I couldn't envision something like that going well.

Before I could voice my doubts, Stone said, "How's the murder investigation going?"

I filled Stone in on what I'd learned about Drago.

Stone shook his head. "Drago's dangerous. Not a good idea to mess with him."

"That's what Ryan said. But the police won't look into Drago, because they're scared of ruffling his feathers. It's up to Ian and me—you know I can't just let it rest. If

Drago's got something to do with Charlene's death, I'm going to find out about it."

Stone looked at me, and his eyes twinkled with amusement. "I've never known you to back down from a challenge."

I watched him warily. "So you're not going to discourage me from talking to Drago?"

"I would if I could, but I pick my battles. If you insist on going to talk to Drago, I'll come with you."

I raised one eyebrow. I shouldn't have been surprised. "You know Drago?"

Stone looked off to one side. "I know all kinds of people."

I'd known that about Stone the first time I'd met him—I remembered Elwood warning me off him, telling me that Stone was involved with all kinds of shady criminal types. I didn't want to ask Stone why he knew Drago, but I was curious. "And Drago won't mind if you come along with us?"

Stone looked at me and raised one eyebrow. "Drago doesn't agree to meet random investigators he doesn't know. He knows me. If I give him a call, he'll agree to meet us."

My heart surged with hope. "And you'll give him a call?" And then I remembered that it was dangerous for Stone to come out of hiding. "But what about Eli?"

Stone shook his head. "Eli knows better than to mess with Drago. As soon as I'm done here, I'll call Drago, and set up an appointment."

"Thank you!" I wanted to rush over and give Stone a big hug, but just then, there was a knock on my door.

I opened it quickly, and Tariq and Ian stepped inside.

"I wanted to give you a progress update," Stone said to Tariq. "Johnson is getting in touch with his people—we should be all set to head to DC next week or the week after."

Tariq nodded. "That sounds good."

"I think we should stop hiding from Eli. If he wants to have a chat, we can talk."

Tariq raised one eyebrow. "I do not think he will want to 'chat.' I think he'll want to kill me."

Stone looked at his friend seriously. "I think the same thing. But we'll never know until we try."

If Tariq was bothered by Stone's plans, he didn't show it. Instead, he just tilted his head. "It is nothing we cannot handle."

Stone looked at me. "I'll send you a text, and we can meet in front of Drago's office."

And with that, Stone jammed his wig and baseball cap back on his head and headed out.

CHAPTER 19

*I*an was over the moon when I told him that Stone would help us arrange a meeting with Drago.

"That's just like Stone!" he said. "He's always the guy to turn to when you need something."

"But what if Drago turns out to be the killer?" I didn't mean to sound worried, but I couldn't help it. "In that case, we could all get into trouble—and then it wouldn't just be Eli gunning for Stone."

Ian flicked one hand dismissively. "Stone knows how to take care of himself! And I'm sure this guy Drago owes Stone a favor or two, otherwise he wouldn't agree to meet us so easily."

265

I tried not to think about what kind of favor Drago might owe Stone, and a few minutes later, my phone beeped with an incoming text. It was a number I didn't recognize, and I assumed Stone had gotten a new burner cell phone, because the message simply said, "5 PM today."

"It's a good thing my shift starts after midnight today," I told Ian. "If we meet Drago at five, then hopefully, he'll agree to talk to us for half an hour or so. We can try to get in touch with Charlene's former roommates again after that, and then maybe we could even try to talk to Brad or Chris."

~

Before we knew it, five o'clock arrived, and Ian and I were stepping out of my car in front of Drago's office.

The address I'd had on file was near the airport, a three-story building that looked like it had seen better days. But the windows were all tinted dark, and it was impossible to see inside. The front door seemed to be made kind of heavy metal or wood, painted white, and I just knew that the place would have bunker-like security inside.

We had only been standing in front of the office for a minute or so, when Stone stepped out of a small black Honda. He was still wearing his blond wig, fake mustache, and baseball cap, and his dark eyes were at odds with the rest of his disguise.

He led us to the front door and pressed a buzzer.

When the buzzer was answered by a harsh, male voice, he said, "It's Stone."

The door was opened by a muscular man with dark brown hair and a short beard. Tattoos ran all the way up the sides of his arms, and he had a teardrop tattoo under one eye. He nodded wordlessly at Stone, and glanced at Ian and me.

We followed the tattooed man inside, up a set of stairs, and into a small room that had been set up like any other office—there was a large desk, filing cabinets, and fake potted plants.

It all looked fairly normal, other than the two burly men who stood behind the desk, arms crossed over their chest.

The man I knew from his pictures as Drago sat behind his desk, and he stood up to shake hands with Stone.

He had a shaved head, sharp, angular features, and piercing blue eyes. His skin was tanned, and I noticed a small tattoo near his wrist. He looked almost like any other businessman, with a white shirt rolled up to the middle of his forearms, and dark, formal trousers.

Stone introduced me and Ian, and we shook hands in turn—Drago's grip was strong, and he looked each of us in the eye.

He sat back down at his desk, and the three of us sat on chairs on the other side. I noticed that the man who'd led us up to the doorway was watching us from his position there.

"Stone said to me you wish to ask a few questions," Drago said, looking at Ian and me. His words had a faint trace of an accent that struck me as being Eastern European, and his eyes seemed to miss nothing. "How can I help you?"

I decided to plunge straight in. "We're investigating the murder of a cocktail waitress, Charlene Nelson. Did you know her?"

Drago smiled, a small polite smile. "You have to be more specific than that."

"I've got a picture on my phone," I said, and handed it over to him.

He studied it for a few seconds, and then he shook his head. "Never seen her in my life."

He handed it back to me, and I put it away, feeling slightly unsure of myself. "Are you sure?"

Drago shrugged. "Maybe she served me drinks once or twice, if you say she was a cocktail waitress. But I have never talked to her, nor do I know her on a personal basis."

He sounded awfully sure of himself.

I said, "But you know her brother, Brad Nelson."

Something flickered in Drago's eyes. He exchanged a glance with the man standing in the doorway, and then looked back at me.

"I know Brad Nelson," he said, steadily. "He is a business partner of mine."

"You own a laundromat together," I clarified.

Drago spread his arms out in front of himself in acknowledgment. "What does that have to do with this waitress?"

"Brad was Charlene's brother."

Realization dawned on Drago's face. And then he laughed shortly. "So you think, because I'm business partners with the dead girl's brother, I had something to do with this girl's death?"

I shifted uncomfortably in my seat. Put like that, it seemed slightly ridiculous. I began, "I was just wondering…"

Drago held up a hand to stop me. "What time did this girl die?"

"Sunday, between seven PM and nine PM."

Drago grinned at me, revealing gleaming white teeth. "I can set your mind at ease. On Sunday night, I was at dinner with my business associates at the Whoosh Steakhouse."

He glanced at one of the men standing behind him. "Isn't that right, Vlad?"

Vlad nodded. His eyes were dead, and looked past me at some spot on the wall. "I was there with Drago."

I looked back at Drago. "You were there the entire time?"

Drago smiled happily and leaned back in his seat. "Of course. Any crime that happens, I always have the perfect alibi."

His words made me shudder. Of course his "business associates" would always vouch for his alibi—no wonder he could never be charged with anything.

I was at a slight loss for what to talk about next. He denied ever knowing Charlene, and he'd volunteered an airtight alibi all on his own. "Would you mind if we asked about you at Whoosh?"

"Not at all," Drago said. His tone was warm and friendly, but his smile was chilly. "Be my guest. I am sure they will tell you I was there."

"And you're sure you've never met Brad's sister? Did you ever hear him mention her?"

Drago looked at me seriously. "I do not attend all business meetings personally. I have only met Brad once—and he certainly never mentioned his sister at that time. Now, if we're done," he stood up, "I have urgent business matters to attend to. Stone, as always, it's been a pleasure."

Stone and Drago shook hands, but the man didn't shake hands with Ian or me.

We all trooped downstairs, and I breathed a sigh of relief once the heavy front door closed behind us.

Stone said, "Even with my disguise, I don't want to be seen here right now. I'm taking off. You two headed to Whoosh?"

"Yes, do you think Drago will mind?"

Stone raised one eyebrow. "Didn't you hear what he said? He's always got the perfect alibi whenever a crime takes place."

"Does he own Whoosh?"

"Yes. But I'm sure Drago had nothing to do with this at all—if he'd been involved, he wouldn't have shaken my hand when saying goodbye. He would have been more annoyed by your poking around."

"What we saw in there wasn't annoyance?"

Stone looked at me in amusement. "That was Drago being downright nice and friendly."

CHAPTER 20

*I*an and I headed over to
Whoosh. The place turned out
to be a cozy steakhouse with dark wood
floors, well-spaced out tables, and private-
looking booths. It was early evening, and
the dinner rush hadn't started.

Security cameras blinked at us from the
walls, but when I introduced myself and
asked the manager if I could look at the
surveillance tapes, he'd shaken his head and
said that was privileged information.

Ian and I asked the wait staff if they
remembered seeing Drago at dinner on
Sunday; unsurprisingly, they all said yes. I
wondered if they'd been told to say so, but
the manager watched us and glowered the

entire time, so nobody wanted to chat for too long.

Ian and I were just about to leave, when I peered into the kitchen, where I could see chefs making salads and other dishes.

My eyes met with those of a blond man busily chopping up lettuce. He grinned and waved at me, and I smiled back happily. Ian and I headed into the kitchen, where I introduced Ian to my old high school buddy, Chad.

"What brings you two here?" Chad said.

"I'm a private investigator now," I explained. "And I'm looking into a man's alibi." I left out the bit about the man in question being the restaurant owner—and the fact that his manager was probably one of his henchmen. It was amazing how many family friendly-looking businesses had links to criminal activities.

"Who's this guy you're looking into?" Chad said. "Maybe I remember him."

I showed Chad Drago's photo, and he nodded. "Yeah, he was here, and he left at seven thirty."

My pulse quickened. "Are you sure?"

"I wouldn't forget it. The man rushed through the kitchen and out the back entrance, as though he was going somewhere in a hurry."

"You're absolutely sure of this?"

Chad nodded. "It's not every day some customer rushes through the kitchen and leaves by the back door. Most people don't even know we've got an exit through here."

Ian and I thanked Chad for his help, and then we headed out to the bar, where we ordered soft drinks, and settled in to think.

I didn't want to say anything out loud, where we might be overheard by one of Drago's employees, but I couldn't help shaking the feeling that Drago was somehow involved in Charlene's death.

Perhaps Drago hadn't been the one who stabbed Charlene—but maybe he had ordered the stabbing, or maybe he'd been around when it had happened. I wasn't convinced that Drago's friendliness proved his innocence.

I glanced over the dining area as I sipped my drink. And then, I noticed a familiar face.

Chris sat at one of the small tables, talking to a young man with curly hair and dark spectacles. The two men were drinking cocktails and laughing. As I watched, Chris gently touched the other man's arm.

I nudged Ian, and he glanced over. We waited 'til the curly-haired man got up, leaving his drink on the table—presumably to go to the bathroom.

When Ian and I showed up at his table, Chris scowled at us, and said, "Can you please not bother me when I'm out?"

"This will only take a minute." I pulled up a chair and settled down at his table. "We'd really appreciate talking to you about Charlene. You did meet her once or twice."

Chris stared into his drink and shook his head. "I'm busy right now."

"I'm sure you've got some time before your boyfriend comes back," Ian said. "But I thought you and Brad were together?"

Chris was silent for a few seconds, and then he looked at Ian. "It's none of your business who I'm with or who I'm not with."

"Maybe Brad would care," I mused out loud.

Chris laughed. "Brad doesn't care one bit."

His tone was so lighthearted that I believed him. "Then why won't you talk to us about Charlene? We understand Brad is upset, but it's no skin off your back to let us know what you thought of her. Why are you being so secretive?"

"I'm just respecting Brad's wishes," Chris muttered. He took a large sip of his drink, and then glared at Ian and me. "I hate private investigators. You guys do nothing but dredge up trouble."

Just then, Chris's companion showed up. Chris stood up abruptly and threw some bills down on the table. "Let's get out of here," he said to the man. "Time to hit some clubs."

Ian and I watched as the two men walked out of the restaurant. Chris turned to say something to the man, who laughed.

Then they were out of the door, and out of our sight.

"That's interesting," Ian said. "I'd

suspected he was gay, but I hadn't really been sure."

I nodded. "But just because he's with a man who's not Brad, that doesn't mean he's got anything to do with Charlene's death."

"He said we could tell Brad about the other man if we wanted to. Maybe we should do that."

I thought it over for a few seconds. "Maybe Chris and Brad are in an open relationship. The laundromat will still be open. Let's go over there, and see if we can find Brad by himself. Maybe we'll get lucky tonight, and finally convince Brad to talk to us."

CHAPTER 21

When Ian and I turned up at the laundromat, we found a number of cars parked in front of the bar and the Mexican food place, but the laundromat itself was empty. The washing machines and dryers were silent, so I assumed nobody would show up to claim their freshly laundered clothes. To add to our good fortune, Brad was sitting by himself at the desk in the back.

He looked at us sadly when we walked in. "I remember you two," he said. But he didn't sound angry, so I decided to push my luck even further.

"Ian and I were hoping you'd spare a

minute or two for us," I murmured, trying to sound understanding and sympathetic. "We know you're going through a very difficult time, but you love your sister so much, don't you want to bring her killer to justice?"

At that, Brad dropped his head into his hands, and let out a soft groan.

I gave him a moment to get himself together, and then he looked up at me. "Charlene didn't deserve what happened to her."

"Then tell us what you know," I urged. "Anything you could tell us, anything at all, would be very useful."

Brad shook his head, and his face closed down. "I can't talk about my sister," he said, his voice sounding as lifeless as his eyes looked.

"I understand how you're feeling." I tried to buy time, not wanting Brad to dismiss us immediately. "Let's talk about something else. What about Chris? Ian and I ran into him at Whoosh. He was there with another man."

Brad looked at me, his eyes tinged with surprise. "So?"

"You're not surprised he was there was someone else?"

"No. He was probably there with his boyfriend, Alexander."

It was Ian and my turn to be surprised. "You mean, you're not Chris's boyfriend?

Brad cracked a smile for the first time. "No, of course not! Chris and I are business partners, no more. I prefer women."

Light dawned. So that's why Chris had said that we could tell Brad about the man we'd seen him with, and hadn't been concerned about being found out.

And then, I remembered the conversation Mary had overheard between Charlene and Chris. "But Charlene told Chris she would tell everyone, and that it was better for you in the long run if the truth came out. If you and Chris weren't secretly dating, what was Charlene talking about?"

Brad's smile disappeared, and he crossed his arms over his chest. "I can't talk about this. If Chris finds out I've been talking to you—"

Just then, the door to laundromat opened, and we all turned around to face the newcomer.

"I warned you to stay away from Brad," Chris said, narrowing his eyes at us. "Why are you two here?"

"You said you didn't mind if we told Brad we'd seen you with someone else," Ian countered. "We thought we'd take you up on that."

Chris looked at Brad. "You haven't been telling them anything, have you?"

Brad shook his head.

"Good."

"You can talk to us," I said, trying to sound friendly and approachable. "We already know you two are in business with Drago."

Brad's jaw dropped, and Chris glared at us. "That's not true."

"We've already talked to Drago, and he just told us that it is. You don't need to hide it from us—we're not with the IRS, and we don't care about finance stuff."

"Get out," Chris snarled. "Don't poke your noses where they don't belong."

I held up my hands placatingly. "I'm not interested in your business dealings. I just want to talk about Charlene." I turned to Brad. "We're not interested in your business at all."

But Brad looked away, and refused to meet my gaze.

Chris tapped his foot, waiting for Ian and me to leave, and I took a deep breath. It wasn't the tack I wanted to go, but I seemed to have no other choice.

"Look, we'd appreciate your help, but if you'd rather not talk to us, we can just go to the police. We can tell them everything we've learned. I'm sure Drago would be happy to know that you're talking to the police about his business interests."

"You wouldn't dare," Chris said in a low, deadly voice.

I shrugged. "I don't have anything to lose. We're only interested in Charlene's death, and if you don't want to talk to us, you can talk to the police."

Chris narrowed his eyes and stared at me for what felt like hours. Finally, he shrugged and walked calmly over to the desk. He pulled open a drawer, lifted out something, and pointed it at me.

I stared into the barrel of a gun.

"I'm not talking to the police," Chris said steadily. "I'm not talking to anyone."

Ian and I took a few slow steps backward.

"Okay," I said. "Let's all stay calm. You don't have to talk to the police. We'll just leave now."

"I don't trust you," Chris growled. "You're going to turn around and head straight to the station. I can't have that. I'm not about to get on Drago's bad side, and I'm not going to give up all the profit we've made so far."

"So Drago's giving you a cut?" I racked my brain, trying to think of some way to placate Chris.

"That's none of your business."

I looked at Brad, but he was busy staring at his shoes. "Brad, I'm not interested in your business. I know that Chris won't talk to us, but I know you loved Charlene very much. It'll make you feel better if you talked to us about her."

"Charlene was—" Brad started to say, but Chris cut him off.

"Don't tell them anything!"

Suddenly, Brad's pupils flared, and he gave Chris an angry shove. "I'll talk about my sister if I want to."

Chris glanced away from us for a second to glare at Brad. "Don't be an idiot."

"It won't hurt to tell them that she was a lovely person, who didn't deserve what happened to her."

"We can't trust them. What if you can't stop talking? I don't need anyone running their mouths."

"I'm going to talk about my sister if I want to!" Brad shouted. "She was a great kid, and I should never have helped you in the first place. I should've just gone straight to the cops—I can't live with this guilt!"

Chris took a step back, and gave Brad a long, hard look. Slowly, he turned the gun from us to Brad. "Okay, then. If you can't live with the guilt, I'm happy to help you die."

"I should never have trusted you!" Brad

yelled. "You killed my sister, and I should never have helped you cover it up."

Chris smirked. "Too late."

The shot rang out, echoing loudly in our ears.

Brad screamed and crumpled to the ground.

Ian and I sprinted over to Chris. Just as he turned and pointed the gun at Ian, I thrust my leg up in a high Rockette kick, making contact with Chris's hand.

The gun flew out of his hand. Chris turned to look for it, and Ian lunged, toppling him over. I added my weight, pinning Chris to the floor, and Ian sat down on him heavily, making sure he couldn't escape.

Brad's loud groans echoed in the small laundromat. I fished a pair of cuffs out of my bag, and cuffed one of Chris's wrists to the table leg.

When I was sure Chris wasn't going to get up, I scrambled over and grabbed the gun I'd just kicked out of Chris's hand.

Finally, I looked over at Brad. His face

was pale and sweaty, and blood pooled where he lay.

I rushed over to him, while Ian kept an eye on Chris.

"Are you okay?"

Brad groaned in response to my question, while I felt for a pulse.

"It hit my stomach," Brad grunted, "Hurts like hell. But I'll be ok. If I get to a hospital."

Brad's eyes were bright and alert, and his pulse was normal. I let out a sigh of relief.

"I'm calling the cops," I told him, "and an ambulance."

Once I'd made the calls and asked for help, Brad turned to me with watery eyes. "I should never have done it," he moaned. "I never knew Chris could be so violent."

"It's okay," I said, "Why don't you rest while the ambulance gets here? You're bleeding out. You don't need to talk."

"But I want to talk. I need to tell someone." Brad groaned again, trying to shift his weight off the wound. "When Charlene threatened to tell everyone we were involved in money laundering, Chris said not to pay her off, and that he would fix things," he said in between grunts. "I thought he meant he would convince her otherwise—but then he showed up with her dead body. He said if I didn't help out, if I didn't say we'd hung out together all night, he'd tell everyone I'd gone mad and killed her, and that I was in as deep as he was."

"You *were* in as deep as me," Chris growled from the floor. "Don't tell these people any more. You're being an idiot."

"No," Brad said. "I'm not being an idiot. I'm doing the right thing, for once. I'll tell everyone what happened. Then maybe I'll stop feeling like I took the knife in my own hands and killed my baby sister. She wanted a comfortable life, and she was a bit silly, but she didn't deserve what happened."

"You can make it right," Ian said, "You can tell the cops the truth."

"That's exactly what I'm going to do,"

Brad said, his eyes glowing with a combination of determination and pain, as the wail of sirens grew closer. "I'm going to finally talk about my sister, and what happened to her."

CHAPTER 22

A week later, I was at my shift at the Treasury. As I dealt out the cards, and made light banter with the three balding middle-aged men sitting in front of me, I thought back briefly over the last few days.

Two days ago, Ryan and I had gone on a quiet dinner date, and in between catching up on our lives and indulging in a delicious three-course-dinner, he'd told me everything that had happened after Brad and Chris had been arrested.

Brad had turned state's witness, and he was helping the police with their inquiries —not only had he turned on Chris, he'd also turned on Drago.

"He felt so guilty about everything," said Ryan. "I believe him when he says he never wanted to get involved in money laundering at all—it was all Chris's doing. Chris manipulated Brad into agreeing to this, and said they would stop after just a few transactions.

"But the transactions kept going, and then somehow, Charlene found out. She wanted money from them to keep quiet, and Brad said he didn't mind sharing some of the money with his sister, since he wanted to see her happy. But Chris wouldn't allow it, and then finally, when she got too insistent, he killed Charlene so as to shut her up forever. He convinced Brad that it was the only way, and that Brad needed to protect him and keep everything a secret."

"So, Drago really never had anything to do with Charlene," I mused out loud.

Ryan shook his head. "No, but Brad met a couple of his henchmen and has shared who they are. Now we can slowly circle round Drago's operation, and with Brad's info, we take him down once and for all."

"So, that's two criminals down in one go."

"Hopefully. And I owe it mostly to a beautiful, meddling PI who doesn't keep her nose where it belongs."

I felt my cheeks growing hot. "Well... you know I can't help that."

Ryan laughed, a deep belly laugh that made my insides tingle. "I know. You can't stop 'til the truth's out there, and I love that about you."

I leaned forward and gazed into his sparkling gray eyes. "So you don't mind that I'm a PI? And that we might cross paths at work every now and then?"

"No, I don't. I only ask that you stay safe. Stop having to fight off people with guns. And maybe don't break into people's homes, or get Nanna to impersonate an officer."

"I didn't—I don't—she was only impersonating a receptionist!"

Ryan's body shook with laughter and took my hand in his. "Okay. But I'm only buying that logic because I can't stay away from you."

～

*B*efore I knew it, my shift was over. I clapped my hands out, said goodbye to the gamblers, and let the new dealer take over my table. I headed out of the bright lights and feverish excitement of the casino pit and into the employee changing room.

As I changed out of my uniform and into jeans and a sweater, I fretted that I hadn't seen Stone in the last few days. He'd come over to chat with Tariq earlier in the week, but I hadn't seen him since.

I felt sure that he and Tariq were hatching a plan to fix everything, and I didn't want to ask them about it. I'd seen no sign of Eli or any of his men, but I thought I could sense their presence.

Billy was still hanging around the casino, too. She'd only approached me one more time, asking me if I'd change my mind, but I told her I hadn't. I didn't need anyone else helping me out, and I especially didn't need an inexperienced blonde who'd seen too many spy movies trying to have some fun and getting herself hurt in the process.

I'm not sure if Billy had gotten the message or not—I still saw her every now and then, and I wasn't sure what she was up to—but I assumed she was harmless, and she'd soon get tired of trying to convince me to let her be my sidekick.

As I headed out of the casino, I noticed Ian waiting for me in the lobby. He was slouched down in one of the low, comfy armchairs, watching people coming and going, and when our eyes met, he jumped up and came over.

"You don't have to wait for me every night," I said. "The case is over, and I'm sure Eli and his men have better things to do than follow me around."

"I'm not about to take a chance," Ian said. "Besides, meeting you at the casino gives me an excuse to get out of the house. Your next-door-neighbor, Mrs. Weebly, keeps telling me that I look like a bum. Maybe it's because I don't get out enough."

I eyed Ian warily. Mrs. Weebly was a bit harsh with the truth, and though Ian's hair was slightly longer than what Mrs. Weebly would approve of, I didn't think his appearance merited such acrimony.

"Even if Eli wanted to have a word with me, I'm sure I could take care of myself," I said. But for a moment, I felt a strange hesitation.

Eli wasn't a run-of-the-mill criminal; he was a mastermind who'd been involved in illegal arms dealing while working for the CIA, and he'd managed to hurt someone as capable and competent as Stone. I wasn't sure that a mere human like myself could take Eli down if I needed to.

Ian didn't say anything about my comment, but he did tell me that he'd won fifty dollars at the roulette table. "I guess that means I can buy some more cupcake supplies," he said. "Now that we finally wrapped up the case, I'd like to try to make those fancy red velvet cupcakes. You know, with red velvet batter, and white icing, and fancy little heart-shaped sugar sprinkles on top."

"That does sound delicious," I agreed. "Maybe I could help you make them too. I did mean to practice my baking skills when I had a free moment."

Ian and I chatted happily about baking for a few minutes, as we walked toward our apartment. But every now and then, I turned and looked over my shoulder.

"What's wrong?" Ian finally asked. "You keep looking behind yourself. Do you see someone?"

I shook my head, no. "It's just this feeling—I can't shake it. Like someone is following me."

Ian frowned. "Let's go home a different way today," he suggested, and I agreed.

"Everyone keeps saying I should avoid that dark alley behind the Cosmo hotel. Let's try finding somewhere that's better lit."

So Ian and I gave our usual route a miss, and instead, we turned onto a side street I'd never been down before. I made another turn, heading toward my apartment, and I was slightly disappointed when I found that this small side street wasn't as well-lit as I'd expected it to be. Sure, it had one working streetlight, but two of the streetlights were dark, and the one on the far end flickered, turning on and off and giving the whole place an eerie, horror movie like feeling.

"This is worse than the alley I usually go down," I muttered under my breath.

I stopped suddenly. Next to me, Ian froze.

"Are those footsteps?" he said.

My heart raced wildly, and my palms felt sweaty. I glanced behind myself, but I couldn't see anyone.

There were cars parked on either side of the street, and I peered at them, narrowing my eyes and taking deep breaths.

"I can't see anyone," I said.

"There!" Ian pointed at the far end of the street.

Two large, hooded figures were walking toward us slowly.

"We can turn and run," Ian said.

He spun around, and was about to race off. But then, my gaze sharpened, and I recognized the two people.

I grabbed Ian's arm. "No! It's just Stone and Tariq."

Ian turned around, and let out a loud sigh of relief. "Tariq and Stone! What are they doing here?"

"I thought they would be hiding out in your apartment," I grumbled, and we walked forward rapidly to meet them.

Tariq and Stone didn't look happy to see us.

"What are you doing here?" Stone said.

"Stone told me that you two take a different way home," Tariq said. "We did not expect to see you here."

"We thought we'd try a new route," Ian said. "We thought someone might be following us."

Stone narrowed his eyes at Ian. "Are you sure?"

"We might have been imagining it," I said, trying to lighten the mood. "But what are you two doing here? I thought you would be in hiding."

"It's taking too long," Stone muttered.

"We thought we would try to draw out Eli and his men," Tariq admitted. "We cannot go to Washington DC unless we know that we are safe, and we will never know that until we talk to Eli."

My heart leaped into my throat. "So you mean, we might run into Eli and his men right here?"

"Don't worry about it," Ian said, his words a symphony of high-pitched fake enthusiasm. "I'm sure Eli and his men would be no match for the four of us. Besides," he said, pointing at a button on his shirt, "I'm wearing that mini spy camera. Maybe we could trick him into saying something that would incriminate him."

Stone and I exchanged a glance.

"This is a bad idea," Stone said. "I don't want you two getting into trouble. You go ahead to the apartment, and Tariq and I will wait here a bit, before coming after you."

I was about to protest, but Ian said, "Stone's right. We don't want to mess up their grand plan."

Tariq nodded. "It is better if it is just the two of us."

I wondered if I should insist on staying,

but I wanted to make Stone's life easier, not more difficult. I thought about Billy, and her insistence on trying to "help" me, and how much I disliked that. I didn't want to turn into that.

In the end, I shrugged, said, "Good luck," and started to walk away with Ian. I could feel Stone's eyes on me, as we headed away, and I told myself that I was doing the right thing. We had only gone a few feet forward, when a movement from behind one of the parked cars opposite where Stone and Tariq were standing caught my attention.

Ian and I whirled around at the same time. We were just in time to see Eli emerging from behind one of the parked cars.

I froze.

Eli was holding a deadly looking gun in his hand, his gray eyes glittered in the darkness, and a thin, amused smile was pasted on his face.

"Stone, Tariq," he said, "how nice to have the gang back again."

I stood there, unable to move,

wondering if I should rush forward and try to save Stone and Tariq. But my legs seemed to be made of lead, and my voice dried up in my throat.

"Eli," said Stone steadily. "What an unexpected surprise."

Next to me, Ian let out a loud squeak.

Eli turned his gaze to Ian and twisted his lips. "And of course, you two are here."

"Leave Tiffany and Ian out of this," Stone said. "They've got nothing to do with it."

"Oh, that's not true," Eli said. "I would've liked to not meddle with them, but you're the one who dragged them into this. You had the brilliant idea of stowing Tariq with a civilian."

A growl escaped from Stone, but he said nothing.

"I wanted to get to Tariq alone," Eli went on, "But it seemed impossible. These two were always around. It's a hassle, but I've decided to be efficient and deal with you all at once."

"Come, now," Tariq said in a mild voice, "There's no need for this."

Eli turned his stony eyes toward Tariq. "You," he snarled. "Why couldn't you just rot in Kabul with the rest of your friends?"

I saw Tariq stiffen. "And let my friend Stone also 'rot?'"

Eli's eyes glimmered. "You always did have a sense of humor. Too bad. After all we've been through, all that I did to shift the blame to Stone. You were the one to mess it up. Where's the flash drive?"

"What flash drive?" Stone said.

"Don't play dumb," Eli warned, "I can get my files the easy way, or—" he swiveled the gun slightly so that it was facing me, not Tariq—"the hard way."

I gulped. I wanted to say something, explain that I had no idea where these files were, that I had nothing to do with it all. But the air was heavy with silence.

And then Ian said, "You know, Tiff told me you got out of Kabul at just the right time."

Ian sounded surprisingly calm, and Eli glanced at him curiously. "That's more than you need to know. Once I'm done with you lot, and the files are destroyed, I can get back to my normal life."

"As opposed to your previous life?" Ian asked. "When you supplied American guns to the Russians and the Taliban in Kabul? And God knows what other information?"

Eli's eyes snapped angrily. "Enough! We don't need to sit around chatting about my past."

"Oh, come on," Ian said cheerfully. "If you're going to kill us, why not explain how you brokered all those deals and made your fortune?"

"Because I choose not to," Eli said. "It's in the past, and no-one needs to know. Now, where's the flash drive?"

"At my place," Stone said. "Let Tiff and Ian go, and I'll get you the drive."

Eli shook his head. "That's not how it works. Tiffany comes with me. The rest of you, scram. I want to see you all walking backward slowly." We did as he said and trudged slowly backward. "Now Tiffany, you walk forward slowly. I'm taking you with me as collateral until I get my drive."

I took a few steps forward, and stopped

a car-length away from Eli. Thoughts raced through my mind, but I couldn't process them. I vaguely felt I shouldn't have come this way. I wondered if Eli would kill me. He most likely would. A man like Eli wouldn't want to leave behind evidence of his wrongdoings.

I wondered if my family would miss me. I wondered if my body would be found in the desert like Charlene's. What would happen to Ian, Tariq and Stone? Eli probably had a plan to get rid of them. I couldn't let that happen! I wondered what I could do to overpower Eli. If I tried to rush him he would shoot me, and then Stone—that's why Stone had said the drive was at his house.

And then, my mind was bereft of all the conflicting thoughts. I felt clearheaded. I could breathe normally again. I saw Eli as he was: a calculating, ruthless man. He'd planned all this out. If I went with him, he'd kill me, and after that, everyone else.

But at least if I went with him, the others would have time to run away or go into hiding.

It was okay. It would all be worth it.

Eli smiled at me. I knew he'd read my mind. Except he had other plans for making sure he was safe.

"Good girl," he said softly. "You don't want me to shoot you, or your friends here." He jerked his head toward a nondescript white van parked just behind him. "Get in here and we'll go."

Still pointing the gun at me, he slid open the door of the van. The inside of the van was a murky darkness, an empty space with a dusty-looking floor. A bundle of what looked like explosives sat in the far corner.

I shuddered and took a deep breath.

I turned around and glanced at my friends one last time. Tears were welling up in Ian's eyes, and Stone and Tariq looked stoic. When I met Stone's dark eyes, he nodded slightly.

Hope surged in me. He had a plan! He must have a plan. Maybe he'd follow the van after we drove off. He'd track Eli somehow. He'd do something to make sure we were all safe.

I smiled at the trio bravely, and stepped up into the van.

Eli raised one hand to close the van's sliding door, and then we all heard it.

A blood-curdling scream. From right behind us.

Eli froze for a second, not moving. And then, pointing the gun steadily at me, he twisted his head just for a moment to glance back. But he was too late.

A bundle of purple clothes and purple-streaked blond hair flung itself on top of him, and a shot rang out. I heard it rico-cheting against the van, and I leaped out and straight onto Eli's back.

I grabbed hold of his wrist. I was twisted instinctively, pulling, trying to angle the gun away from my friends. Billy landed a swift kick somewhere in Eli's nether regions. Eli toppled over, with me anchoring him face-down on the ground.

And then everyone was around us.

The gun was dislodged from Eli's hand. Tariq and Stone cuffed Eli's wrists and Stone appropriated the gun. Ian hauled me up and in for a teary-eyed embrace, and as we hugged, Billy sat on the ground near Eli, clasping her knees, and sobbing.

A few long minutes went by. The world seemed to whirl round too quickly, everything was in chaos and only Tariq and Stone were calm. Eli was ranting, struggling to get out of the cuffs. He hurled out threats and curses, until Stone pulled out a stun-gun, hit the button loudly, and Eli fell silent.

I took a deep breath, pulled away from Ian, and grabbed Stone for a big hug, tears suddenly streaming down my cheeks. Stone stroked my hair, and I noticed Ian and Tariq approaching Billy and trying to calm her down.

"You w-were going to let me go with him," I sobbed, my fear and adrenaline suddenly replaced by an unexpected anger. "He was going to kill me and then he was going to kill you!"

Stone continued to stroke my hair and held me close. "Nothing of the sort. Johnson's parked a street over. We'd have called Ryan straight away, to make sure he'd pull Eli over in a squad car and get you out."

My tears stopped and I stared up into Stone's dark eyes in surprise. "You were— Johnson was right here?"

"A street over. He didn't see Eli coming, but we've texted him to get here now."

"So… you would've told Johnson to follow the van. And then Ryan to stop him."

"We'd need to involve a cop. Eli wouldn't mess with an officer."

I felt the tears streaming down again, this time from relief. I leaned in to Stone. His chest was strong, and his arms warm as they wrapped around me.

In my silence, I heard Billy sniffling, telling Ian and Tariq that she was okay now. She'd followed us, she explained, and until Eli pulled the gun, she'd thought we were all friends. And then she'd crept up behind him and attacked. "I wanted to help you guys," she said, looking up at Ian, "I didn't mean for anyone to get hurt."

"Nobody got hurt," Tariq reassured her. "We are grateful for your help."

A sleek black car drove up silently, and Stone let go of me as Johnson parked and stepped out.

"We've got Eli right there," Stone said, jerking his head toward the prone body. "He'll come to in a few minutes."

"I'll take care of him," Johnson said. "I know some folk who'd like a word with him. What exactly happened?"

"I've got it all on tape," Ian said, beaming proudly. "I knew my spycam would come in useful!"

He ripped off the button-like camera and handed it over to Johnson. "I can text you my server login so you can watch the whole video."

Johnson pocketed the tiny thing, and he and Stone exchanged an amused glance.

CHAPTER 23

*J*ohnson and Stone tied Eli's ankles together with thick rope, and then they lifted Eli's prone body into Johnson's car.

"He'll be safe with me," Johnson said, "At least 'til I tell my CIA contact to haul his butt over here and sort things out."

My heart lifted at his words. *Sort things out...* So things would get sorted out soon! It was all worth it—just to clear Stone's name from the blacklist Eli had entered it onto.

Johnson, Tariq and Stone chatted in low voices for a few minutes, while Ian and I thanked Billy for her help. She was still sniffling, explaining she'd never thought someone would attack us with a gun. "I can't believe this all happened," she said. "He would've killed you!"

"I would've been fine," I said, smiling cheerfully. I glanced over at Ian. His eyes were still worried, and I gave him a quick squeeze on the shoulder. "My friend Stone had it all figured out. But it's a good thing we didn't need his plan after all!"

Billy sniffed, and rubbed away a tear with the back of her hand. "I can't…" And then she peered at me closely. "You don't even seem that scared!"

I sighed. "I've been through this kind of thing a few times now. Hazards of the job."

Billy shuddered. "Then I'm staying away from this kind of job. It's not for me."

"That's okay." My voice was sympathetic and I gave Billy a quick hug. "You were there when it counted."

"Do I have to go to the cops or make a statement or something?"

I glanced over my shoulder at Stone, who still talking with Johnson and Tariq, and then back at Billy. "Do you want to?"

Billy shook her head rapidly. "No, no. I don't like dealing with the cops. And you try to help someone out and they hit you with an assault charge." I remembered what I'd seen on her record. "I can't go through that again. I'd rather not. I mean, do I have to?"

"No. You don't."

Stone and Tariq came back to join us, and we all watched as Johnson drove off silently. Long after the car had disappeared, the five of us gazed off in that direction, each lost in our own thoughts.

"Well," said Stone, breaking the silence finally, "we should get home."

"Goodbye," Billy said. "I won't see any of you again. I'm off to LA tomorrow—I'll try to get a part on TV."

"Good luck," I said. "Are you sure you're feeling well enough to head back home by yourself?"

Billy nodded. "I'm staying in a room at the Treasury. I'll be fine. I hope you—" her voice tremored a little—"I hope everything works out for you guys. And I hope that

315

man trying to shoot you gets what he deserves."

"I'm sure he will," said Stone. His face was a grim mask, and his eyes were narrow.

CHAPTER 24

*I*an and Tariq disappeared into Ian's apartment, and Stone and I stood before my door.

Stone peered at me carefully. "You feeling okay?"

"I'm fine. I'm just glad Eli's with Johnson. How come he came to the alley alone? I thought he'd always have men around himself."

"Didn't want witnesses."

I shuddered and looked down. "He really meant to kill me, didn't he?"

Stone didn't answer for a moment. And then he said, "Doesn't matter what he wanted. I would never let anyone hurt you."

Something fluttered in my heart.

I looked up and into Stone's dark, stormy eyes. His gaze locked onto mine, and for a moment, I felt time stand still. He placed one hand on my lower back, and stepped closer, close enough for me to feel his strong, powerful aura.

"I'm glad you're back," I said softly.

"Me t—"

A door flew open loudly behind us, and the noise of footsteps shuffling forward broke the spell. I turned around, and almost bumped into my neighbor, Mrs. Weebly. She was staring at Stone, her smile a beacon of delight.

"Stone!" she said. "I haven't seen you for so long! Did those horrible men who were looking for you, leave?"

"Yes ma'am," he said. "They're gone for good."

"And they won't be around again?"

"No, ma'am."

Mrs. Weebly's voice flooded with relief. "I'm so glad." She turned to me. "You must be happy, too."

I smiled, remembering how Mrs. Weebly had warned us of the men just in time. "I'm glad things got sorted out." I turned to Stone again. "They *are* sorted, aren't they?"

"Yes. We've just got to introduce some people to Eli, provide them with the files he hid. I'll stay out of sight for a few more days, and then we'll all go to D.C. and sort things out officially."

"And life's going to be back to normal after that?"

"Life's going back to normal."

Stone nodded goodbye to Mrs. Weebly, and gave me a sudden, unexpected wink.

I watched as he turned and disappeared into the elevator.

Stone was gone again, but this time, it was okay. He was back in my life, and the truth about his past was all getting sorted out.

Life was going to be back to normal.

No, better than that—life was going to be good.

EPILOGUE

a few days later, Ian and I met with Andrew at the bar of the Treasury Casino for drinks.

My shift had just ended, and I'd changed back into my usual non-work clothes of jeans and a t-shirt. Andrew was wearing a button-down shirt and khakis, and he sipped his martini morosely, completely ignoring all the happy noises and bright cheer of the casino.

"I really appreciate everything you guys've done," he said, staring into his martini and swirling it around. "I had no idea that Charlene... well, she may have been after a rich man to marry, but she was still my lucky charm."

I smiled at him kindly. "I'm sure she was a good person underneath." I hadn't told him how she'd been quite nasty to some of the people she worked with, and that in my opinion, once she'd snagged her "rich husband," she'd revert to her usual mean self and take it out on him.

Andrew sighed. "And now she's gone… and so's my luck!"

"What do you mean?" Ian said.

"Well—when she was around, I was lucky, I was winning things, I was getting upgraded for free. But now she's gone, I'm not lucky any more. I don't win any of the games, I don't find lucky quarters… I don't think luck even exists now that my lucky charm's gone."

I felt a shiver race down my spine and I looked at Ian, wide-eyed in recollection. "Billy told us she could be our lucky charm."

Ian's jaw dropped as he remembered that conversation. "She did—and she was."

Andrew snorted. "No such thing. I don't know what you're talking about exactly, but—hang on, is this Billy still around?"

I smiled and shook her head. "No, she left for LA. And... I'm not really sure she's a lucky charm. I mean, we were very lucky when she showed up, but my friend had a plan all along even though we didn't need it."

Andrew's shoulders drooped and he took another sad sip of his martini. "Well, I guess that's that. I'm flying out tonight, and then I'm at work from tomorrow— back to my usual self. Back to my usual life."

I smiled. "Except maybe once a year, when you come back to visit Vegas?"

Andrew's eyes crinkled. "Maybe. Maybe I was wrong about Charlene being my lucky charm. Maybe my lucky charm is Vegas itself."

"You've got a point," I said slowly. "Living in Vegas has been pretty good for me."

"Me too," chimed in Ian, finishing his beer and standing up to say goodbye to Andrew. "We'll see you when you come to Vegas again."

As Ian and I walked slowly home, the

chat with Andrew hung heavily in the air between us.

Lucky charms might not exist, but the people you surrounded yourself with could make your life feel like one big lottery win.

Made in the USA
Coppell, TX
08 April 2021

53330773R30194